THAT SON OF A GUN FROM LINCOLN COUNTY

"I'm running this spread now," the man in the red shirt said to Rae Marsh. "And we ain't hiring. Neither are we free lunch for grubline tramps. You git one meal, with the crew, an hour from now. Then you're on your way."

Rae Marsh drew in a long angry breath. "I'm part owner of this ranch and I don't figure on leaving in a hurry."

Red Shirt dropped his hand to the level of his holster. "The hell you say, stranger. You got two minutes to get off this land. Now—git!"

But what the man in the red shirt did not know was that you can't talk like that to a pardner of Billy the Kid, fresh from Lincoln County. Not if you want to stay above ground!

BROTHER BADMAN

Ben Elliott

CHARTER
NEW YORK

A Division of Charter Communications Inc.
A GROSSET & DUNLAP COMPANY
51 Madison Avenue
New York, New York 10010

An ACE CHARTER Book

I

RAEFORD MARSH had come a long and weary way from New Mexico, and it showed on him and on his travel-gaunted bay. Of the two of them, the bay looked better—it could live on grass. But a grubline rider without four bits to jingle in his pockets could go hungry between ranches and line cabins, unless he could knock over a deer or an elk or a few rabbits with sixgun or rifle. Rae Marsh had seen little game, so he was whittled down to skin, bones, and stringy muscle by the long ride.

But now it was coming to an end. He had been seeing Circle M beeves all morning, and the spread below him in the valley—the cluster of log buildings and the three corrals, in one of which there was horse-breaking going on—that should be the Circle M home ranch.

It was the place he had come all this way to find, but he did not start down to it immediately. He kept the bay reined in on the pine-covered slope, hooked one leg around the saddle horn, tilted back his hat, and used the last of the makings in his Bull Durham sack to build a cigarette.

Marsh was a man just edging into his mid-twenties. His shaggy brown hair was straight where it worked down over his ears below his flat-crowned sombrero. His face, dusted with freckles underneath, wore a tan deep enough to make him look Indian. His nose was short, almost snub, his mouth wide and usually smiling faintly. Dismounted, he would not have been quite six feet tall. In flannel shirt and fringed chaps, there was nothing to distinguish him from any other drifting puncher of his age—except his eyes.

Those eyes were a little slanted beneath heavy brows, and they were a peculiar brilliant blue. They were the first thing you saw when you looked at his face, and they had been the last thing on earth four men on the Murphy side of the Lincoln County War had seen in this life.

And yet they were not warlike eyes, nor was the cedar-butted Colt on his hip worn in warlike fashion—it was hitched high for riding comfort. But the eyes were cool, intelligent, and now they missed no detail of what was going on down there in the Circle M horse corral. A lineback dun bronc had just tossed a twister sprawling into the dust. Then Rae Marsh sat up straighter in the saddle. The twister was scrambling out of the dust and running for the rail as the horse came after him. Just in time, he made it over. The dun slammed into the fence with an impact Marsh could hear all the way up the hill. But what made him lean forward and stare was the fact that the red-shirted bronc rider had run into a nearby bunkhouse and now was coming back, and he had a rifle in his hand.

Marsh unhooked his leg from around the horn and slipped a foot into the stirrup. He pulled the bay's head up and jigged it down the hill.

But he had only gone a couple of dozen yards

when he saw the red-shirted man climb the corral
fence and perch on the top pole. The dun horse,
curveting around the enclosure, spied the man,
reared and whinnied, and charged him again, neck
straight out, teeth bared.

The red-shirted man waited a second or two until the horse was nearly upon him. Then Marsh
heard the bark of the rifle and the dun went spinning sideways and crashed to earth, dead. The red-
shirted man nodded, jacked another shell into the
chamber, and climbed down off the fence. He
strode toward the bunkhouse, followed by a couple
of punchers who'd been watching. One puncher
went into the corral to drag the saddle off the dun.

Rae Marsh frowned. All right, the horse had
plainly been a man-killer, and there wasn't much to
do with such an animal except rub it out. Nevertheless, he was a little upset by what he had just
witnessed—it seemed almost a bad omen. Or maybe somewhere in the back of his mind he knew that
most killer horses were made, not born, and usually made through cruelty, and that he might expect
to find some of that down on the Circle M.

All the hands who had been watching the fight
between man and horse had drifted inside the
buildings when Rae rode into the ranch yard, except for the two who were saddling mounts in a far
corral, preparatory to dragging the carcass of the
dead dun away from the main ranch. They looked
at him curiously as he reined in before the rambling
log building that was the ranch house.

Marsh paid no attention to their stares. He was
busy appraising the layout of the Circle M. Obviously it was a prosperous spread—all its build-

ings were staunch and spacious, its corrals repaired and in order, everything recently whitewashed. That tallied with what he had seen of its cattle; somebody had been breeding up the ordinary range beef with Hereford and Shorthorn blood—something rarely seen on spreads not owned by any of the big Eastern or English syndicates. *Whatever else a man might say about him,* Marsh thought, *he knows his business.*

Stiff with riding, he swung down off the bay and knotted its reins about a hitchrack before the house. He was a little surprised, as he mounted the steps to the puncheon-floored veranda, at how his heart seemed to have stepped up its beat, at the knot of anticipation and eagerness in his belly. This was a day he had dreamed of for years, ever since he had been old enough to understand the story the Clintons had told him. But he hadn't really known until now just how much he had looked forward to it, how much it meant to him. He had been in gunfights in which he'd been less keyed up.

"Hello, the house," he began through a throat dry with tension, but before all the words were out, the door had swung open in response to the clomping of his boots.

The man in the red shirt, the one who had killed the horse, stood in the doorway. He was a big man, an inch or two taller than Rae Marsh; maybe five years older, and far heavier. His shoulders were wide and sloping, his head so big it reminded Rae of that of a bull buffalo. A thick shock of black hair hung down over his forehead. Beneath heavy black brows, his eyes narrowed as they took in Marsh's travel-stained figure.

"Yeah," the man in the red shirt said tersely. His

voice was deep, truculent.

Rae fought down an odd, instantaneous dislike of Red Shirt. He kept his tone as pleasant and even as he could. "Morning," he said. "I'm looking for Mister John Marsh."

Red Shirt leaned against the doorjamb, and his face went completely expressionless. His eyes were nearly slits now.

He took his time about answering. Finally he said, "He ain't here."

Rae felt a cold fear growing within himself. He licked dry lips. "Where is he? When'll he be back?"

Red Shirt's mouth twitched at one corner. "He ain't coming back."

Rae Marsh stared at the man a moment. "What do you mean?" he asked softly at last.

Red Shirt straightened up. "I mean," he said, "he's dead. We buried him three days ago."

Something seemed to collapse within Rae Marsh, to slump and die. After all these years, after so much waiting, so much hoping, and then getting the letter and pushing the bay as hard as it could go— He just stood there, looking at Red Shirt blankly while he tried to master the grief and disappointment that threatened to overcome him.

"So I'm running this spread now," he heard Red Shirt say, as if from very far away. The man took tobacco from his pocket. "And we ain't hiring. Neither are we any free lunch for grubline tramps. You git one meal with the crew, an hour from now. Then you're on your way." He had opened the sack and sifted tobacco into a cigarette paper and swung the sack between his teeth by the tag and string. Now, contemptuously, he focused his attention on the cigarette he was rolling.

Marsh fought down the impulse to jerk the sack out of the man's mouth. "I'm not a grubline rider," he said quietly.

Something in his voice made Red Shirt look up, and when he saw Rae's eyes, he pulled away from his leaning position against the doorjamb and stood up straight. Slowly he took the tobacco sack from his mouth and stuck it into his shirt pocket. Then he put the cigarette between his teeth.

"Then who are you?" he asked coldly.

Rae Marsh drew in a long breath.

"I'm John Marsh's son," he said.

There was an interval then when neither of them said anything. As they looked at each other, time seemed oddly suspended; Rae was conscious of the clang of hammer on anvil in the smithy, the far-off bawl of a bull.

Then Red Shirt took his cigarette from his mouth without lighting it. "The hell you are," he grunted.

"My name's Rae Marsh," Rae said. "And I think we've about reached the stage where you better tell me who you are, too."

Red Shirt's mouth twitched again. "I don't have to tell you anything, buddy. Except this. You take that cock-and-bull story of yours and hightail it off Circle M. Now. You got two minutes to git gone."

"I didn't come here to turn around and leave in two minutes," Rae said, still holding onto his temper. "I came here to see my father. Now you tell me he's dead. I figure you better tell me some other things, too. Like, maybe, how he died and who you are and—"

Before he could finish, somebody came up behind the man in the doorway. "What is this,
Cleve?"

"Git," Cleve, in the red shirt, said without looking around. "It's somethin' I'll take care of."

"I want to know what's goin' on," the man behind Cleve said. He pushed towards the door, and
reluctantly Cleve made a little room for him. Instinctively, Rae Marsh tensed. But when the other
man appeared in the doorway, Rae saw that he was
not quite a man—a boy, sixteen maybe, possibly
seventeen, not older. He was medium height, his
frame had not yet filled out, and he seemed
dwarfed by the big Colt he wore lowslung and tied
down. But what riveted Rae Marsh's attention was
the boy's eyes. They were like his own—blue and
slightly slanted. "Who is this fellow, anyway?" the
boy asked, running his eyes up and down Rae.
"What do you want, mister?"

"I want some names first of all," Rae said quietly. "And I want to know what happened to John
Marsh. I understand you buried him this week."

"You said something crazy a minute ago," the
boy said. "If I heard you right—"

"I said my name was Rae Marsh and I'm John
Marsh's son." Rae could hear his own voice losing
its control, beginning to quaver as anger and grief
and disappointment roiled up within him. "I rode
a long way to find my father and now you tell
me—"

Something came over the boy's face. He was
staring at Rae's eyes, just as Rae had stared at his.
"Well, I'll be damned," the boy said. All at once
his face broke into a grin. "Cleve, this is what Dad

meant when he said—"

"Shut up!" Cleve barked. "Dammit, keep your big mouth shut!"

He took a step forward, coming up close to Rae.

"All right, friend," he said tautly. "I'm Cleve Anders. And this is my half-brother, Will Marsh. Now I don't know what kind of sandy you're trying to run, but it won't wash. John Marsh left Circle M to me and Will, share and share alike. Now you come in here with a big windy about—"

"Wait a minute, Cleve," Will Marsh began.

"Dammit, I told you *hush!*" Anders roared. "I'll handle this!" He thrust his face close to Rae's. *"Hombre,* you got one minute to take this confidence game of yours an' git! And I'll tell you now, if you set foot again on Circle M, you won't live no longer'n it takes a cap to pop—you *sabe?"*

Rae could take it no longer. He stepped back a pace. He was hardly aware that his hand had moved—certainly neither of the two men before him saw it move—but suddenly his gun was out, pointed squarely at Cleve Anders' belly.

"Judas!" Will Marsh breathed. "I never seen a draw like that!"

"All right!" Rae's voice crackled. "I'm tired of this horsin' around. I come here in good faith and I'm not gonna be choused off like a coyote after the chickens. Back up, Anders—back up and put on your readin' glasses and take a look at this." With his left hand, Rae fished in his shirt pocket and brought out an envelope. He thrust it at Anders.

Anders looked from the envelope to Rae's face and then, slowly, he reached out and took it. "I don't know what's in here," he said hoarsely, "but whatever it is, it don't make any difference."

"Let me see that." The boy took the envelope from Anders. He opened it and extracted a well-worn folded sheet of paper. After glancing at it, he looked at his half-brother. "It's Dad's writing."

Cleve Anders snorted a terse obscenity.

Will Marsh began to read aloud.

" 'My dear son,' " he read. " 'You may not believe you're dear to me, but you are, even though I've not seen you since before you were old enough to walk. Unless the Clintons have told you, you may not even know you are my son.' " Will Marsh lowered the paper and looked at Rae. "Who're the Clintons?"

"Folks used to have a little spread down near Horsehead Crossing on the Pecos," Rae said shortly. "They raised me." He was still holding the gun on Cleve Anders, never for an instant losing his alertness where the big man was concerned.

Will read on. " 'It's too late now to make excuses for my neglect of you. The facts are these: When I came home from the War, I was wiped out in Louisiana. We pulled up stakes and headed for Texas with what outfit I could rake up. Near Horsehead Crossing we got hit by Comanches. In the fight, your mother was killed, most of the rest of my outfit gone. I grabbed you and managed to make a run after dark. Got away, with an arrow in my leg. Don't remember much of the next day. Just remember coming up on the Clinton place. Josh and Henrietta Clinton were good folks. I was about out of my mind with grief for your mother— I loved her more than my own life.

" 'Stayed with the Clintons a month or two. They got along all right with the Comanches— Clinton could talk it. Then, still half-crazy, I had to pull out, go somewhere, do something. That country was no place for a man with a kid not even weaned and no woman to look after him. I left you with them, promised to come back. Like you know, I never did.

" 'Hard to explain why. Couldn't bear to think of your dead mother, and you the greatest reminder of her. Drifted on through to Colorado, picked up a stake hauling to the mines. I've got a good ranch now, Circle M, in a place called Fletcher's Hole, near a town named Bent's Crossing. No time to think about you, about anything but work for couple of years. Then I wrote back to the Clintons, but they'd moved on somewhere, couldn't locate them. While I was trying, I met my second wife, Virginia Anders. She brought me a son from her first marriage and gave me one of my own, your half brother Will. A fine woman, but peculiar in ways. It'd be too long to explain why I never mentioned you to her, but I didn't. And I'm ashamed to say, I stopped looking for you.

" 'But she's gone now, and the doctor says I'm a sick man. There's something growing inside me they can't cut out and it's eating me up. I won't die tomorrow, but I won't live forever, neither. Now I have heard a rumor there's a Rae Marsh in Lincoln County, N.M. I am entrusting this letter to a rider bound there who promised to find that Rae Marsh and deliver it.

" 'If you're the Rae Marsh raised up by the Clintons, you're my son. After the way I've behaved, I don't expect you to think anything of me. But if you will come, I will try to make it all up to you. I want you to meet your brothers and get to know them and join them in running the spread, share and share alike, and when you come I will make a will and put that in it.

" 'I've got maybe three or four months left. That isn't much time to make up for it all, but I should last that long. If I don't, I do hereby devise and bequeath to my firstborn son, Raeford Marsh, one third interest in every worldly good with which I am endowed, being of sound mind and because I love him very much. This letter should stand in court. Please hurry home. Your affectionate father, John Marsh.' "

When Will Marsh stopped reading, there was a brief silence on the porch. Then Cleve Anders broke it with a snort. "If that ain't the biggest pile of crap I ever heard of."

Will held out the letter and turned to his half-brother. "No, it ain't, Cleve. I told you, Daddy said something about—"

"The old man was so doped up," Anders grated, "he didn't even know his own name. It was like that for two months before he kicked the bucket. He was ravin'." His dark eyes bored into Rae's. He had guts, Rae had to admit; he didn't seem at all worried by the gun. "Mister, that's buncombe through and through. Forged letter, made-up story—"

"Cleve, I told you, it's Dad's writing. And his eyes, look at his eyes—"

Anders shook his head impatiently at Will's protest. "I ain't fallin' for it and neither are you. Now, I ain't going to tell you again—let me handle this." His hard eyes met Rae's. "I don't care who you are, you ain't gettin' an inch of Circle M land nor any head of Circle M stock, letter or no letter. This spread's half mine and I ain't splittin' my half with nobody. Now, are you gonna git, or am I gonna have to have you horsewhipped off?"

"You want to try that?" Rae's voice was harsh now, like metal grating against metal. "I want to hear about how my father died, about what he said about me. And I—"

He didn't finish. Behind him, somebody said quietly, "What you'll do is stand hitched, mister, and drop that gun."

Rae stood frozen. He'd been caught up so in the whirl of emotions churning through him that he'd been oblivious to the fact that there were other people on the Circle M besides himself and the two men who confronted him. Now the hard iron of a gun barrel was ramming into his spine.

"Good work, Clyde," Cleve Anders said, his mouth twisting in a grin. He stepped to one side and reached for Rae's Colt. There was nothing to do but let him take it.

"Now," Anders said hoarsely. A triumphant light was shining in his eyes, and he licked his lips with a kind of eagerness. "You think you can threaten me with a gun right smack in the middle of *my* spread? Watch him close, Clyde. If he moves, blow a hole in him." He thrust Rae's gun toward Will. "Here," he said, spraddling his legs, digging in his heels. "I'm gonna teach this booger a lesson. Come in here, pull a gun on me, huh? I *said* I'd whip you off this ranch!"

Before Rae could move or dodge, Anders' big hand swung in a blurred arc. Open-palmed, it

crashed against Rae's face; its impact knocked him
backwards, head full of lights and bells. His
bootheels dug for floor that wasn't there as he went
off the edge of the porch. Then he was flat on his
back in the dooryard dust, dazed and shaken. He
shoved himself to his elbows, vision clearing
enough to see the man who'd come behind him
with the gun standing there grinning, and Cleve
Anders grinning too as he sprang from the porch
toward Rae.

Rae rolled and tried to evade Anders; he was too
dazed to meet the man head on. But he didn't make
it; the big man in the red shirt had him by the collar, yanked him to his feet.

"Dammit, Cleve!" Will Marsh yelled from the
porch. "Give 'im a chance!"

"Chance, hell!" Anders bellowed. There was another backhand blow on its way towards Rae.
There was no way it could miss, and Rae's head
seemed to explode with its impact. Anders was bull
strong, and that second blow knocked Rae half unconscious. He was only vaguely aware, then, of
other blows following it, of his head being battered
back and forth. He sensed rather than felt it when
Anders let him go and he dropped to hands and
knees in the dust.

"Cleve!" he heard Will's voice, seemingly from
very far away.

But then Anders was kicking him. He felt the
hard, sharp boot toe in his ribs, over and over; he
tried to roll away from it, to block it with his arms.
But he had no strength left for evasion; he was
being beaten to a jelly and knew it and there was
nothing he could do about it except lie there and

take it. One shattering rack of pain after another tore through him; he couldn't see, he couldn't breathe.

"For God's sake, Cleve!"

Will Marsh. His half brother. There was scuffling around Rae's head; Will must be trying to drag Cleve away. Then the kicking and the pain stopped, and Rae Marsh was crawling there in the dust, panting, whimpering like a beaten dog, gasping for breath.

Then, bit by bit, his head began to clear: He saw Cleve Anders' spread boots, spurred, before him. There was blood on the rowels—his blood; Anders had used the spurs, too.

Now Anders' voice penetrated the numbed fog that still wisped through Rae Marsh's brain. "All right, saddle-tramp. On your feet." Anders' big hand was jerking Rae up, flinging him like a rag doll against the flank of the bay tethered at the hitchrack. "Mount and ride. What you've just had is nothin' but a sample of what you'll git if you show your face in Fletcher's Hole again, I promise you that."

Dazedly, instinctively, Rae's groping hand dropped to his holster, but it was, of course, empty. "And you ain't gettin' that sixgun back, either," Anders grated. "Now, on your horse. Help him up, Clyde. Looks like he's had a little accident that's bunged him up so bad he cain't even climb up on a horse."

The Circle M hand who had come to Anders' rescue with the gun moved forward. "Up you go, waddie." He hoisted and shoved; Rae lurched into the saddle like a sack of potatoes. He could barely keep his bruised and bloody face, now rapidly swelling, out of the horse's mane.

Reins were thrust into his hands. There was the whack of somebody slapping the bay's rump and the animal skittered into motion. The jar of its gait sent fresh pain shrieking through Rae's body. But he grabbed the horn and somehow managed to hang on as the bay galloped out of the Circle M ranch yard.

Somehow the very pain of each hoofbeat, the rhythm of it, began to clear Rae's head as the bay galloped on. At last he sat up and looked around and gave it guidance with the reins. He headed it for the sloping foothills over which he had ridden this morning, and before long the Circle M was well behind and the bay was panting as it climbed through timber.

When he could finally manage to sit upright, Rae Marsh reined the horse in. Still gasping with sickness from the beating he'd taken. But even more sick inside than outside, he swung the animal around. Through the timber he could just see the Circle M, a cluster of toy buildings like a scatter of children's blocks.

In the center of its yard was a minute speck of red that moved about. Rae Marsh's lips curled back from his teeth.

"Damn you," he said, and his voice was at last full-throated. "Damn you, you haven't heard the last of me yet." He drew in a long breath. "One third of everything down there belongs to me. I didn't care about it before—all I wanted to do was find my father. But I care about it now. It belongs to me, do you hear? And I'll take it, Anders—I'll take it any way I can get it, even if I have to steal it from you piece by piece. You'll remember this day, Anders. You'll remember it a lot longer than I will, I promise you that."

Then he reined the bay around, touched it with his spurs, and rode into the timber.

II

THE SCREAM of a hawk, circling high over the clearing in which he had slept, brought Rae Marsh awake.

It was full daylight and the sun was high. Marsh sat up suddenly, surprised to find it so late—and then he groaned in agony. His whole body was a mass of bruises, as sore as if he'd been thrown and tromped on by a bronc. As the memory of yesterday's humiliation came back to him with full force, his mouth tightened and his eyes narrowed.

He got slowly to his feet, wincing with the pain of it, but, as he moved about and the sun warmed him, some of the pain seemed to abate.

The bay was cropping grass at the edge of the clearing. Near where it grazed there ran a narrow, clear, cold stream, foaming and boiling over sharp rocks.

Rae stripped off his shirt. His torso was gaunt from short rations, but it was layered and plied with plenty of hard muscle. Right now it was mottled black and blue with bruises. He pressed his ribs gently but found no indication of any breakage. Then he went to the stream and washed to the

17

waist in it, snorting and gasping with the shock of
the icy water.

When he had dried, he felt much better and far
less stiff. He slipped on shirt and brush jacket and
realized suddenly that he was ravenously hungry;
he hadn't really eaten since day before yesterday,
when he'd stopped over at that trapper's cabin.
The pangs he felt in his belly were so sharp they
took his mind off his aches.

He stood there thinking about it a moment.
Then he grinned. It was a slow grin that did not
really move his lips much, and it was not a pleasant
thing to see.

Cleve Anders had taken his sixgun, but Anders
had made a mistake and had left the Winchester
saddle carbine, which was still in its scabbard.
Marsh went to it, stroked its stock absently for a
moment, still grinning, then picked up saddle,
blanket, and rifle with scabbard and lugged his
gear toward the hobbled bay.

The Circle M ran a lot of cattle, and it did not
take Rae Marsh long to find what he was seeking—
a couple of fat cows in a brushy ravine, one of them
with a chunky yearling calf.

Marsh had ridden a long way into the timber last
night, but not quite far enough to get off Circle M
range. Nevertheless, he figured he'd put enough
distance between himself and the main ranch for a
rifle shot not to make much difference.

He got off the bay and dropped the plump yearling with a single shot. The cows spooked at the
smell of blood and dashed past him out of the
ravine.

His face set in a grim smile, Rae took his *riata*

off his saddle. Looping it around the yearling's forefeet, he dragged the carcass out of the ravine to high ground. There he skinned it and butchered out a huge, choice steak quickly and with dexterity.

There was plenty of dry wood about, and he built a fire that was almost completely smokeless. By that time, the steak had cooled out enough to cook. While he broiled the meat, he let a spare cinch ring heat to a cherry red in the coals. When he judged it hot enough, he picked it up between two sticks and went to the green hide with it. Several heatings were necessary before he had completed what he had set out to do.

By that time, the steak was ready. He wolfed it down, and when he could hold no more, he felt restored and capable.

He went back to the yearling's carcass and hacked off just about nearly one third of the meat. He cut one third of the green hide off the rest, spoiling it, and wrapped the meat in it and threw the bloody bundle far down into the ravine. The rest of the carcass he left up here on high ground, in plain sight. Soon it would attract vultures, crows and magpies. Also, he guessed, Circle M riders.

All that done, he hung the remaining two-thirds of the hide on a tree above the carcass, mounted up, calculated directions by the sun, and headed toward where he judged the town of Bent's Crossing to be.

Behind him, a rising wind flapped the raw and bloody hide back and forth. The branded message on its hair side was crudely done, but it stood out plainly:

⅔ FOR U—⅓ FOR ME—RM

Cleve Anders, Rae knew, would understand immediately that it was a declaration of war.

It took him a long time to reach Bent's Crossing —not that he had trouble finding it, but he rode with an instinctive concern for cover, keeping himself and the bay off the skyline, his eyes searching the terrain warily, his hand never far from the butt of the saddle gun.

While he rode, he tried to make some sense out of everything that had happened.

He had built up a lot of hopes, a lot of daydreams, on the long ride up here to Fletcher's Hole. There were things that he had never known or had that he had hoped to find here. An end to drifting, a sense of belonging somewhere—and the father he could not remember ever having seen, and now would never see.

The Clintons had been good people, and they had taken the best care of him they could. But they'd had children of their own, too, and somehow Rae had always been just enough of the outsider to feel it keenly. As soon as he was old enough to understand, they'd told him how he had come to be with them, and from that day on he had lived in the constant hope that someday his father would come back for him—his real father. Every rider appearing over the horizon had been an adventure—and a disappointment.

But John Marsh had never come and never written. The Clintons pulled up stakes and moved to New Mexico. The range wars were on, and the Apaches were still out. It was a country where a man had to learn to use a gun to grow up. Rae found that he had a talent for using a gun.

But the Clintons were by nature restless, and once again they moved on, to California this time. When they left, Rae, now fully grown and his own man, stayed behind.

He worked for Chisum for a while, John Chisum, the fabulous cattle baron who branded with a Long Rail and earmarked with a jinglebob. That was when his path first crossed that of a buck-toothed kid named Bonney, who was older than his years and extremely likeable. He and Bonney wound up together again, later on, working for an Englishman named Gerald Tunstall, whom they both greatly admired. When Tunstall was drygulched in cold blood, Bonney swore vengeance; before long he and Rae both were caught up in the swirling cross-currents of that complex, bloody battle which came to be known as the Lincoln County War.

Bonney, it developed, thrived on fighting and killing; Rae saw a new side of him—the boy was cold-blooded and ruthless as a weasel. By that time, Rae was entitled to notches on his own gun if he had chosen to carve them, and his reputation might, in time, have equalled that of the Kid. But the thought of having such a reputation revolted him.

He had already made up his mind to break loose when the rider bearing John Marsh's letter had sought him out.

Rae could still remember the surge of emotion that had gone through him when he had read the letter. It had not been the prospect of inheriting cattle or range that had sent him riding, pushing the bay hard; it had been something far deeper than that, something he could not put into words.

But he had had to find his father before the old man died and the chance was lost forever.

And now he had been too late. The grief in him at realization of that was deeper than anger or the lust for revenge for what Cleve Anders had done to him.

But at least John Marsh had acknowledged him as his son. John Marsh had wanted Rae to have his fair share of the Circle M. That was what mattered now—that the old man's wishes be carried out, not thwarted by Anders, who held half and obviously was determined not to see his share whittled down by further division. All right, he could fight Anders —the big man was no blood kin to either him or his father. But what about the boy, what about Will Marsh? There was no doubt that he and Will had the same father, that the same blood ran in their veins. Will had seemed to sense that, too, had even seemed willing to talk about the matter and work out some kind of settlement. Still, when the chips were down, what would Will do? Would he wind up having to fight his own half brother, too, in order to claim his rightful inheritance? That was a prospect he was not looking forward to.

Bent's Crossing was bigger than he had expected it to be. No river had given it that name; it had received it because it lay at the easiest entrance to Fletcher's Hole and the Bents had once had a temporary fort here to protect their hired trappers from the Blackfeet and Southern Cheyennes who had considered this their hunting grounds forty or fifty years before. The remains of the old fort could still be seen on the flats outside the town, its log palings tilted and full of gaps, its buildings caved and decaying. Beyond it, the town nestled under the shoulders of the mountains, with a wagon road, a good one, leading outward. It was a good-sized clutter of buildings, as towns went in that country, some log, some board. There were no mine-pockings on the mountains behind it, so it must have been built, Rae guessed, pretty much on cattle.

He didn't really know now what pulled him toward it—he knew no one here and there was the price, maybe, of one dinner in his pockets, depending on how high things were. But maybe—just maybe—the town boasted a cemetery, and maybe that cemetery was where John Marsh's body lay. He would find out, anyhow.

By now it was early afternoon, and as he eased the bay onto the hardpacked main street of the place, Bent's Crossing looked deserted; everybody would be eating dinner. He ticked off in his mind the attractions the town had and the facilities it offered: five saloons, a couple of general stores, a butcher shop, a marshal's office, even a small bank. Then he saw what he wanted—a sign jutting from one false-fronted building: *Sam Murney, Gent's Clothes* and, under that legend, another one: *Undertaker*.

He put the bay to the sidewalk, swung down and tied it. A little bell over the door tinkled when he entered the establishment of the versatile Sam Murney. There was one wooden rack of store clothes and some tables piled with Levis and California pants and flannel shirts. At the rear of the store, a very thin, bald-headed man, coatless, but wearing vest and pants to a suit, sat tilted back in a chair with his feet propped up on a fireless iron stove. Crumb-filled papers spread across his narrow lap showed that he was just finishing lunch.

Without any perceptible hurry, he let the chair come down, got to his feet, and stuffed the papers into the stove. Then he came forward to meet his customer, his eyes running dubiously over Rae's worn, scuffed, and dirty clothes, which the tussle in the Circle M yard hadn't helped.

"Howdy," he said. "Somethin' for you?"

"No clothes. Just a little information. Sign says you're an undertaker."

"That's right." Sam Murney's voice was immediately lower, reverent, as if he had switched to his undertaking tone. "We can lay your dear departed out for his Heavenly Journey so natural you would think he was only sleepin' if you didn't know better."

"Uh-huh," Rae said. "What I wanted to ask was, did you by any chance handle John Marsh's funeral?"

Sam Murney looked at Rae with narrowed eyes. Something cautious moved across his face. "You any kin?"

"I'm his son," Rae said. It sounded odd to be saying it aloud that way.

"Oh, you're that one," Murney said, and now his voice had gone definitely hostile. "Yeah, Cleve spread the word about you yesterday afternoon. Mister, maybe you don't want my advice, but folks around here'll tell you it's good. Now, you take my word for it, you're not buyin' yourself anything but bad trouble hangin' around here with that story. Best thing you can do is cut out. The road leads right over the mountains and it ain't a bad ride at all."

Rae felt his temper boiling up. So Anders had been here before him. And apparently Murney was afraid of Anders. Maybe everybody else in town was, too.

His temper was in his voice. "Mister, I didn't ask you about the road. I come in here to find out where you buried John Marsh."

His eyes were full on Murney, and the skinny man saw something in them that made him step back a pace.

"All right," he said, flustered. "All right, don't git your back up. Ain't no skin off my nose if I tell you. We got a graveyard out there behind the old fort. Planted John there, next to his dear, departed loving wife."

Rae let out a long breath. "Thanks," he said tautly. "That was what I wanted to know." He whirled and strode out of the store, unlatched the reins of the bay, mounted and rode back out of town.

Maybe, he thought, he wasn't about to take on just Circle M. Maybe he was about to take on Bent's Crossing, too, maybe even all of Fletcher's Hole. Maybe Anders drew enough water to line them all up behind him.

He was so caught up in his grim thoughts that he didn't notice the rider who had moved out of Bent's Crossing on the same road, far behind him.

Like most frontier graveyards, this one had a forlorn, untended look. Some of the graves had wooden headstones, some tombstones carved out of granite, some no marker at all. But there was no missing the raw, red fresh pile of dirt in the middle of the cemetery.

He groundhitched the bay and went into the cemetery.

The two granite stones were identical. The first one marked the resting place of Virginia Anders Marsh, who had died two years before. The second one, at the head of the fresh grave, said tersely: *John F. Marsh,* and besides the name bore only the dates of birth and death.

Rae Marsh took off his hat and looked down at the raw earth, and he was full of grief for all that might have been and yet had never come to pass. As he stood there, the shadows from the high-palinged walls of the old fort fell across him, for he was there a long time, how many minutes he did not know, caught up in a skein of grieving, bitter thoughts.

Then his reverie was broken as the bay raised its head and nickered greeting to another animal and, instinctively, Rae Marsh sprang into action, whirling toward his mount.

But he was too late. Foolishly, he had left his saddle gun on the bay, and now a rider had pulled up between him and the horse and was looking down on him. Rae froze, but the desperation in him subsided as he saw that the rider was a woman.

She sat her mount sidesaddle. Her figure from the waist down was obscured by the flowing riding skirt. But from the waist up, under her tight bodice, it was something to make a man catch his breath.

She was about his own age, maybe a little younger. She had jet black hair pulled smoothly back behind her ears, a saucy riding hat perched atop its shining coils. Her eyes, in a face untanned by sun, a face pale and smooth and flawless as a lily petal, were black as her hair and very large; now they held an odd expression that was a mixture of amusement and sympathy. Her nose was straight, perfectly chiseled, her mouth full and red-lipped, her chin firm. As she looked down at Rae, her lips curved slightly in a strange smile.

"I'd hoped you were smarter than that," she said. "You let me ride right between you and your horse." Her eyes flicked downward to his hips. "And you're not even packing a handgun."

"There was something else on my mind," Rae said.

"That?" She motioned toward the grave.

"Yes," he said. "That."

"I'm sorry about him," she said. "He was your father, wasn't he?"

"Yes, ma'am," Rae said. "He was."

"It's too bad he went before you got here," she said. "The doctor told me he was surprised it happened so quickly." Her dark eyes roved up and down him boldly. After a moment, she said, "Cleve claims he took your gun away by himself. But I think he must have had help."

"He had help," said Rae.

She nodded again. "Well," she said, "aren't you going to give me a hand down?"

"Excuse me," Rae said. He came forward quickly. She slid down off the horse with the lithe grace of a panther. She was not as tall as he had thought; her head came just to the level of his eyes.

"Thanks," she said, when she was solidly on the

ground. "My name is Gwenn Crystal. Nobody ever calls me Gwenn. Everybody calls me Crystal."

"All right," Rae said. "I'll call you Crystal, too. My name's Rae Marsh."

"I know who you are," she said.

"Everybody does," he said with a touch of bitterness. "Anders has spread the word, huh?"

"You might say he's posted you," she said. "He's made Bent's Crossing off-limits to you."

"He draws some water here, huh?"

"He's been running things since John Marsh got sick. Circle M's the biggest ranch in the Hole. Bent's Crossing was John Marsh's town. But when John came down with what killed him, Cleve stepped in to fill his boots. Now Bent's Crossing is Cleve's town. Everybody was sorry when John died. He was the only one could hold Cleve Anders in check."

"He's a hardcase, huh?"

"You ought to know his style," she said. "You got a dose of it yesterday."

Marsh nodded. "All right," he said. "You know all about me. But I don't know anything about you."

"I told you my name," she said. "I own a place in town." Then her eyes narrowed, her lips thinned. "And nothing would make me happier than to see you take Cleve Anders down and rub his nose in the dirt. In fact, if you want to kill him, I'll buy the bullets!"

Rae Marsh stared at her for a long moment. Then he said quietly, "Lady, I think this is something you and me ought to talk about."

Crystal met his eyes. "I think so, too," she said, and her voice was crisp. "Give me a hand up and we'll ride back to Bent's Crossing."

"You're not afraid to be seen with me?"

"I'm not afraid of anything," she said, and the way she said it made him sure of its truth. "Come on. We'll ride in and talk at my place."

III

CRYSTAL'S "PLACE," it turned out, was the biggest saloon in town, and that was exactly the name it bore: *Crystal's Place*. They rode together up to it along the town's main street, walking their horses. Rae Marsh's head swung from side to side. He was wary as a wolf, now; he'd had two lessons in letting his emotions dull his senses—one yesterday at the Circle M, the other today when Crystal had ridden up on him so easily. His eyes missed no detail along the sidewalks, including the way people whispered together at the sight of Crystal and him riding stirrup to stirrup.

"I saw you ride in," Crystal explained. "Saw you go into Sam Murney's, saw you ride out again. I knew you had to be the one Cleve spouted off about. I was afraid you'd get away before I could talk to you. Or that even if I did catch you, you'd turn out to be some spineless jellyfish."

"We'll see," Rae said. They halted before a hitchrack; he swung down and gave Crystal a hand. Then he took her arm as they climbed the boardwalk and went into the saloon.

It was nearly empty—a couple of solitary drinkers at tables, a half-dozing bartender. "Come

on," said Crystal. She led Rae toward stairs at the
rear of the long, wide room.

His spurs jingled as he climbed the stairs behind
her, his saddle gun in one hand. At the top, there
was a short corridor, a single door.

"This is where I live," Crystal said. She opened
the door. Rae followed her into what seemed to be
the living room of a two-room apartment. It was
furnished well, with a horsehair sofa, good chairs,
a desk, a carpet on the floor, and a crocheted cloth
on the big table in the center of the room.

Crystal shut the door and turned the key in the
lock. "Before we go any further," she said, and she
went across the room to the secretary. She unlocked a lower drawer, fished inside, and turned.

"Here," she said, coming back to where Rae
stood. "No matter whether we strike a deal or not,
you'll be needing this." What she was holding out
in her hand was a long-barreled Colt .45 with an
ivory grip and silver chasing on the cylinder and
backstrap. He saw at once that it was a fine and
expensive weapon.

"It's a loan," she said. "If you pull out, I expect
you to return it first."

Rae took it a little hesitantly. "No better than
you know me, you oughtn't to trust me with something like this."

Her red mouth quirked. "Let's say it's a token of
my good faith. I said I'd buy the bullets; I might as
well provide the gun, too."

Checking it, Rae saw that it was fully loaded.
"All right," he said, thrusting it in his waistband.
"I'll take it on loan. Until I get my own gun back,
or another to take its place. Because I can't afford
to buy one; that's a fact."

"Take good care of it," Crystal said. "It belonged to my husband."

"Oh?"

She looked at him oddly. "Yes," she said. "Cleve Anders killed him six months ago."

Before Rae could find anything to say to that, Crystal turned. "If you're broke," she said, "I guess you're hungry, too." She raised her voice. "Hallie? Oh, Hallie . . ."

The girl who came into the room from another door in response to her summons looked astonishingly like Crystal, but she could not have been over eighteen or nineteen. She had the same black hair, the same great, dark eyes, the same flawless skin. But there was a difference, too. Crystal had a hardness that seemed to suit her name; there was nothing hard about this girl. She was dressed in white, which suited her coloring well, and when she saw Rae, there was a shyness, even a little fright, in her eyes.

"This is my sister, Hallie Blaine," Crystal said. "Hallie, this is Rae Marsh."

"Pleased to meet you," Rae said. Alone, he thought, the girl would certainly be pretty enough, but next to Crystal she seemed to fade, seemed almost plain. She murmured something inaudible in acknowledgment of the introduction.

"Hallie, maybe you wouldn't mind running downstairs," Crystal said, "and asking Hank to send out for steak and potatoes for Mr. Marsh. And to send up a pot of coffee, too."

"All right," Hallie said softly. She did not look at Rae as she crossed the room and went out.

When the door had closed behind her, Crystal sighed. "Hallie's still a little upset," she said. "She disapproves of me. She was living with an aunt in Independence, but Aunt Mattie died and she had to come here a couple of months ago. She didn't know I had this place until then." She gave a short, barking laugh. "She's another good reason why I'd buy the bullet to rub out Cleve Anders."

"I don't understand," Rae said.

"You will," she said. "Drink?"

"I could use one."

"Sit down," she said. "I'll get it."

Rae seated himself on the horsehair sofa. Crystal entered from the other room in a moment with a bottle and two glasses. She poured straight whiskey into both glasses and sat down in a chair across from Rae after handing him one.

"Here's how," she said, and drank hers like a man.

Rae drank his, too. It bit home immediately, for his stomach was empty, and he relaxed a little. "Now," he said, "maybe you'll talk a little."

"All right," Crystal said. "Ward Crystal and I came here five years ago and opened this place. We served honest drinks, ran honest games. My husband was a gambler, Rae, but he was a straight one. You ask anybody in town. They all liked him."

Rae nodded. "Go on."

"When big John Marsh was in his prime, nobody could stand up to him, least of all Cleve Anders. I don't know what Virginia Marsh's first husband was like, but he must have been real scum to leave her with something like Cleve. Just the same, John could handle him. But then John got sick with this tumor or whatever it was he had. Then Cleve started to run wild."

Rae nodded. "He wouldn't have dared come near a married woman," Crystal went on, "while old John was up and about. John would have heard of it and given him a horsewhipping. But after John was down, Cleve decided that . . . that . . ." For the first time her voice shook.

"All right," she said, when she had regained control. "He wanted me. But it so happened that I loved my husband, Mr. Marsh, and I wouldn't give Cleve Anders the time of day—I wouldn't wipe my feet on him. I tried to make that plain to him, but he couldn't get it through his thick head that he wasn't God's gift to women. He thought it was Ward, my husband, standing in his way. And . . . and one night Ward was crossing the entrance to an alley and somebody . . ." She hesitated, gulped for breath, but there were no tears in her eyes. "Somebody," she said harshly, "shot him through the head from out of the dark."

"And you're sure it was Anders."

She stood up, went to the bottle, and refilled their glasses. Her hand, he noticed, was shaking a little. "I'm sure," she said. "Nobody else is. There wasn't any proof, of course, not a clue as to who'd done it. But I know."

"Is Anders still hanging around you?"

"I think he realizes that I know. And I think he's finally got it through his head that I wouldn't touch him with a ten foot pole. But . . ." She gestured toward the door. "There's Hallie. It's only a matter of time before he starts after her. The minute he does," she finished harshly, "he's a dead man. If I have to kill him myself."

She turned towards Rae. "Anyway," she said, "that's why I rode out to find you. If you're here to make war on Cleve Anders, you've got a partner."

"I'm here," Rae said, "to get the third of my father's ranch he willed me. I owe Anders a good stomping for the stomping he gave me. But I don't owe him a killing." He stood up, rubbing his hands along his legs as if they were sweaty. "I had enough of killing down in Lincoln County."

"Don't be a fool," Crystal said sharply. "Do you think Anders is going to give up a square foot of Circle M to you without you having to kill him?"

"There's the courts," Rae said. "I've got a long-hand letter from my father . . ." He touched his shirt pocket; the envelope was still there. Will Marsh had handed it back to him just before the gunhand had got the drop on him.

"The courts," Crystal snorted. "It takes money to fight a case through the courts." She paused. "I've got money for the man who makes war on Anders, who hurts him bad. But I've got no money for court fights that he'd probably win anyhow."

"I didn't ask you for money," Rae said. "I can get money."

"How?" Her face registered disbelief.

Rae had been thinking about it. His mouth quirked. "It's simple. All I got to do is sell as much of my share of the Circle M stock as it takes to finance the lawing."

Crystal stared at him. "What?"

Rae shrugged. "One third of Circle M beef and horses belongs to me. Only way I can raise money is take 'em and sell 'em."

Crystal was silent for a moment. Then she said, in an odd tone, "You mean rustle 'em."

"I don't consider it rustlin' to take what rightfully belongs to me."

Crystal was silent a moment more; he could almost see her mind working. Then she gave that short, barking laugh.

"If they catch you at it, they'll hang you."

"That's a chance I got to take," Rae said simply.

Crystal sat down. She rubbed her hands together. "It all comes to the same thing," she said at last. "You do that and sooner or later you'll have to kill Cleve Anders or he'll kill you." She looked suddenly very happy. "You can't do it alone," she said. "You'll need some men. You'll need a place to hide the stock while the brands are being changed. You'll need contact with a buyer."

"I'll find all that somehow," Rae said.

"Maybe I can save you some trouble," Crystal said.

"You know somebody?"

"There's a man owes me a favor," Crystal said. "A couple of favors. If I write him a letter—" She broke off. "You'll have to take it to him in person. He won't work with you unless he likes the way you size up."

"I'll take it to him," Rae said.

"It's quite a ride," she said. "He's got a place down in the brakes along the Colorado River, almost at the Wyoming line. That's a good hundred miles from here."

"What's his name?"

"Tom Ford," she said. "And he runs with a tough crew. He knows people in Wyoming and Utah who'll buy your stock."

"Sounds like a man I can use," Rae said.

"I'll give you the letter. And a stake for grub and cartridges. You'll have to strike your own terms on the money from the beeves with him."

"I appreciate it," Rae said. "One more thing."

"What's that?"

"This kid out there at Circle M. Will Marsh. He's my half brother. What about him?"

"He's not dry behind the ears," Crystal said. "He's only seventeen. If you're looking to him for help, forget it. Since he's a minor, Cleve's his legal guardian. And the way Will's going, he's not going to live to be twenty-one."

"What do you mean?"

"Did you see the way he wore his gun?"

"Yeah. I saw it." Rae recalled the lowslung Colt on the kid's hip, the tied thigh-strap.

"He's gun-crazy. You know the kind. Maybe he's a good enough kid, probably is, but he can't think about anything but that gun he wears. Old John held him down, just like he held Cleve, but now Will's loose to tote that gun anywhere he wants to. He's out to build himself a reputation. You can just see him itching for trouble every time he comes to town. Nobody's given it to him yet, but someday he's going to meet up with the wrong man and that's going to be the end of Will Marsh."

"The damned little fool," Rae said, feeling oddly saddened.

"I think Cleve encourages him in it," Crystal said. "After all, if anything happened to Will— why, then, Cleve would own *all* of Circle M."

"But he hasn't killed his man yet," Rae said.

"No."

"Somebody ought to knock some sense into his head."

"Who's going to try to, when he's itching to use that gun?" She shrugged. "He's misguided, full up on stories of people like Billy Bonney and John

Hardin and the like. In time, he'd grow out of it. But he'll get himself killed before that happens."

"I can't let that happen," Rae heard himself say. "He's my half brother."

Crystal's voice was harsh. "You'll be lucky if you're not the one he picks to go up against. Cleve Anders may be a skunk, but he's no fool. You go to war against Circle M and Cleve will work on Will. He'll talk Will into going up against you if he possibly can. Either way it comes out, Cleve'll be the winner."

There was a knock on the door. Then the girl, Hallie, entered, bearing a tray with coffee and cups. "The food will be along in a little while," she said, her voice soft, shy. She tried hard not to look at Rae as she set down the tray.

"Thanks, Hallie," Crystal said.

"You're welcome." The girl crossed the room and disappeared through the other door.

Crystal's sharp voice brought Rae around. He realized suddenly that he had been staring at the door Hallie closed behind her.

"All right," Crystal said. "If you want my help, you get that look off your face."

Rae felt blood burning under the skin on his cheeks. "I didn't have any look on my face."

"She's not going to get mixed up with anybody like you," Crystal went on coldly. "No more than I would let her get mixed up with Cleve Anders. Get that through your head now."

"I told you—" Rae burst out. Then he bit it off. "Let's have some coffee," he said.

"All right," she said. "You have your coffee and your grub, when it comes. I'll have a bath fixed for you—God knows you could use one. Then you get some sleep." She indicated the sofa. "After that, if you mean what you say, you'd better be riding for Tom Ford's place."

"I mean what I say," Rae told her.

"Meantime," she said, "stay off the streets of Bent's Crossing. I don't want you to get what Cleve Anders gave Ward."

"Thanks," Rae said dryly.

"Not until you've served your purpose, anyhow," Crystal said, with a tight smile, and then she poured the coffee.

IV

FOR THE LAST half hour, Rae Marsh had been riding taut in the saddle, skin prickling with almost unbearable tension. The trail he was on was hardly a trail at all; it was a hellish jumble of rocks through the mixture of heavy forest and tormented badlands that marked the margin of this loop of the Colorado where it swung from Wyoming into Colorado before thrusting on back into Utah. He had passed the last landmark Crystal had told him about, a high mesa with a shaprly slanting top far to his right, and now he was deep in owlhoot territory. At any moment now Rae was due to be challenged by a lookout—or, just as easily, he might be dropped by a shot from ambush. It would all depend on how edgy Tom Ford and his men were.

Still, there was nothing for it but to keep on—

A rifle bullet screeched off a rock just under the nose of the bay, and the animal sat down on its haunches. The report of the gun slammed and echoed through the rock jumble that filled this place. Rae Marsh came instantly back to reality.

His first impulse was to dig for his Colt. He checked that just in time, knowing it would be his last move. Instead he fought the scared bay with his left hand, the reins tight-gathered, and held his right high in the air.

His eyes swept the great piles of boulders and eroded earth. There was no sign of anyone, not even a wisp of powdersmoke. "Hello, up there!" Rae bawled. "Don't shoot." His voice echoed and re-echoed through the badlands.

Only after the last tag of it had died did an answer come. "Mister, turn around and ride out."

"I can't," he yelled back. "I've got to see Tom Ford!"

There was only silence, during which the echoes died. Rae kept on probing rockpiles with his eyes, saw nothing. Then the voice bellowed: "What you want with Tom?"

"I've got a letter for him from Gwenn Crystal in Fletcher's Hole!"

Another silence, while the unseen gunman thought that over. Then: "All right. Drop your gunbelt. Climb down off that hawse and stand out rein's length away from that saddle gun."

Rae lost no time in obeying. When he had carefully lowered the silver mounted sixgun to the rocks in its scabbard and was at the full length of the reins from the bay's head, there was a clatter of rocks. A man in a ponyskin vest and a flat-crowned gray hat appeared from behind a tower of rock thirty yards away, leading a sorrel horse. There was a carbine cradled under his right arm and its muzzle never wavered from Rae. His face was beardy and suspicious.

"What's your name, stranger?" he growled as he came up.

"Marsh. Rae Marsh."

The man's black brows grew together. "I've

heard that name. You . . . let's see . . . you ever in New Mexico?"

"Lincoln County," Rae said.

"You ever know a man named Hobbs? Boots Hobbs, they call him."

Rae stiffened. "I know Boots Hobbs. Why?"

"Nothin'," the man said. "What you want with Tom?"

"I told you; I got a letter from Crystal. And a business proposition for him."

The man stooped, picked up Rae's gunbelt without ever taking his eyes from Rae or wavering the rifle-bore. Then he went to Rae's saddle and fished the carbine from its scabbard.

"Okay," he said. "Mount up. We'll ride in."

"You don't take any chances, do you?"

"Ain't paid to," the man said.

They rode for three miles more, into a narrow defile clogged with loose rock and down timber. They passed two more guards, rounded a corner where the narrow canyon twisted, and as the guard beside Rae reined in, Rae drew in a breath of surprise and admiration.

Before them stretched an immense, grassy flat. In the center of it was a cluster of log buildings and corrals that could have been the main station of any wilderness ranch. Beyond, almost lost in haze, was the rim of a great canyon—through which, Rae knew, the narrow Colorado snaked, making an approach from the rear impossible. For an outfit on the owlhoot, it was, he thought, an ideal place, ranch and fortress combined.

The man beside Rae rubbed his beard. "I been thinkin'," he said. "This Boots Hobbs. He was on the Murphy side of that fight, wasn't he?"

"That's right," Rae said. He began to feel a certain strange apprehension. Why did this fellow keep bringing up the name of Boots Hobbs? Hobbs had been one of the most brutal of as brutal a crew of gunmen as anyone could have gathered. He had not been smart, but he had been fast with a gun, lightning fast. He was known for his cruelty and his gunspeed and known, too, for being able to drink an incredible quantity of liquor without it affecting his draw.

"And you was on the McSween side."

"I guess you could say that."

The beardy man chuckled.

Rae looked at him sharply. "What's so damned funny?"

"Oh, nothin'," the beardy man said. "Only it's liable to be real interestin' down there tonight. Your friend Boots Hobbs rode in two days ago. He's been likkerin' up ever since. And braggin' that one of these days there's two men he's gonna git. One of 'em's this Billy Bonney. The other one"— he paused, savoring the joke—"is a feller named Rae Marsh."

Rae let out a long breath. All at once, gunless, he felt naked. Now that he was out of that Lincoln County mess, he had nothing against Boots Hobbs, though he detested the man. But he knew Hobbs' mind didn't work that way. To him, Rae would still be an enemy, somebody to be shot on sight.

He turned to the beardy man. "Listen," he said. "If Hobbs is there, I can't ride in without a gun."

The beardy man did not look concerned. "That's up to Tom," he said, and he gestured. Following the direction of his hand, Rae saw a man riding toward them across the flats.

They rode to meet him, and as they drew together Rae could see that Tom Ford was a very tall, very thin man, wearing a high-crowned hat in the fashion of the northern ranges. As he came up and reined in his black horse, Rae saw that his face was cadaverous, hollow-cheeked and big-nosed and long-chinned, his mouth a slit, his gray, intelligent eyes deepset in their sockets. He wore his Colt hung low, and his hand rested on its butt as the black skittered to a halt.

"All right, Mace," he said in a surprisingly deep voice. "What you got here?"

"Says he's Rae Marsh from Lincoln County," Mace said. "And got a letter for you from Crystal over in Bent's Crossing."

Ford's gray eyes went up and down Rae. "Marsh, huh? From Lincoln County? And you know Crystal?"

"She says you owe her a favor or two. And I got a proposition for you. Might let you pay her back and make some money at the same time."

"The letter," said Ford, holding out his hand.

Rae fished it from his shirt pocket and gave it to Ford. The thin man put the reins between his teeth and ripped open the envelope. He read for a moment, brow corrugating. Then he visibly relaxed. "All right," he said to Mace. "Give him back his iron." He looked at Rae a moment longer. "Marsh from Lincoln County," he said thoughtfully, as if to himself. Then: "Did Mace tell you about our company down yonder?"

"Boots Hobbs," Rae said, buckling on the gunbelt Mace handed him.

"Yeah," Ford said. He looked at Rae's gun.

"Ain't that Ward Crystal's hogleg?"

"It was," Rae said. "Crystal loaned it to me."

"I'll be damned," Ford said. "I've tried to buy that off Crystal three times and she wouldn't sell. Then you come along and she just hands it over. . . ." His mouth quirked, and in that moment he looked less like a corpse, almost human. "Women," he said, and then he sobered. "You listen here," he said. "I don't make up my mind quick. We'll have to do some talking before I give you an answer about what was in Crystal's letter. Meanwhile, there's Hobbs." His voice went harsh. "I think he's a drunken, loud-mouthed bastard. He rode in two days ago bound for the Tensleep country and he's long overdue to get gone. I'm sick of the sight of him. But you're on your own with him. He's mentioned your name, made some big talk against you. I expect he'll brace you, sooner or later, if he ain't all wind. I don't give a damn if you kill him or he kills you, but I'll tell you this. Me and my men are out of it completely. You don't hafta worry about us helpin' Hobbs and he doesn't have to worry about us helpin' you. *Sabe?*"

"*Sabe,*" Rae said, tight lipped. "I'm not looking for trouble. If Hobbs leaves me alone, I'm not out after his hide."

"Maybe he'll leave you alone," Ford said. "But I doubt it. Anyhow, that's between you and him. Come on. Let's ride in."

The main building of Ford's layout contained only one large room. Its walls were crude bunks; the rest of its furnishings consisted of a stove and a couple of big tables with benches.

Four hours had passed since Rae had entered

this place, and with each minute that ticked away his nerves had drawn more taut. When he had come in, a group of men had been playing poker at one of the tables, and Rae had instantly recognized Hobbs as one of the players. He was a big, blocky man with the face of a bulldog, perpetually surly and frowning. He wore two guns, ordinary range clothes, and the knee-high kangaroo-skin boots that had given him his nickname.

When Rae and Ford had entered, the group at the table had looked up. Hobbs, raising a glass of whiskey to his mouth, froze with the glass just missing his lips.

"You boys meet Rae Marsh, from Lincoln County," Ford said as they halted just inside the door. "Rae, this is Charlie Flannigan, Mac Jenkins . . ." His voice droned on, reeling off names. Rae neither listened nor looked at the men introduced. He was keeping his eyes on Hobbs.

Hobbs just sat there with the liquor glass high, staring at Rae, a snaggle-toothed grin playing across his face.

". . . And I b'lieve you know Boots Hobbs," Ford finished, irony in his voice.

"Yeah," Rae said. "Hello, Boots."

Hobbs was still grinning. "Howdy, Rae. Where did you come from?"

"Same place you did," Rae said quietly.

"Everybody comes to Tom Ford's," Hobbs said. He and Rae stared at each other for a long minute. Then, as if Hobbs had made a decision, he turned back to his cards, tossing off the drink in his glass. "Awright, dammit," he said. "Who was it opened?" The card game picked up, but the voices of the players were muted, and Rae could sense the tension in the room as each man, expecting trouble, gathered himself to get out of its way in a hurry when it broke.

But so far it had not broken. Hobbs seemed to have made up his mind to ignore Rae's presence. Rae and Ford sat and talked, but Ford would not get down to business. It was as if he were waiting for something, waiting for Rae to produce some additional credentials of some kind before he would take Rae seriously.

Rae had no appetite for talk himself. If Hobbs seemed unaware of his presence, he was certainly not unaware of the presence of Hobbs. He never relaxed for a moment.

Then, far into the evening, the poker game broke up, and now Hobbs was scraping back his bench. He had been drinking steadily, and he seemed to be very drunk; he reeled and wobbled as he stood up and, very ostentatiously, stretched. He had, Rae noticed, apparently been losing heavily.

"This ain't my night," he said thickly. His boots clumped on the floor as he lurched across the room toward the table where Ford and Rae sat alone. Rae heard a kind of sighing in the room as Hobbs came toward him, a tense chorus of indrawn breaths.

He swung off the bench to face Hobbs. His hand was away from his gun, but not far.

Hobbs grinned. "You don't hafta look like a damn' cornered lobo, Rae," he said. "I ain't comin' after ya. Jest wanna buy you a drink an' talk about ole times. We're outa Lincoln County, now." He walked around the table and sat down on the far side, next to Ford, across from Rae. He folded both hands on the table. "Them was wild days. You remember when we burned up the McSween house? Thought we had you then, you and Bonney and that Mex, but you shot your way out and got over that damned wall—"

"Yeah, I remember," Rae said.

"I hear Governor Wallace is still tryin' to get Billy to accept a pardon." Hobbs shoved Rae's untouched glass toward him. "That your'n? Hell, man, drink up and I'll buy you another'n. We got a lot to talk about."

"I ain't thirsty right now, Boots," Rae said quietly. "No offense."

Hobbs shrugged. "Okay," he said. "None took." He turned to Ford. "Tom, I got to buy another bottle. Lemme see if those sharks of your'n left me the price of one." He leaned back as if to dig into his pocket and his left hand went off the table.

That was when Rae had to make a decision and make it in the flick of an eyelash. His own hands had been on the table, in full view. Now, either Hobbs was going for money—or he was going for his left gun.

He made his decision. He did not draw. Instead, with lightning speed, he threw himself from the bench. Just as he did so, Hobbs' gun roared under the table and a bullet shrieked through the space where Rae's belly had been.

The rest of it happened, then, in less than two seconds. Hobbs, looking startled, raised his gun above the table. Rae, off balance, drew and fired. It was a chance shot, a snapshot, as he was still hurtling sideways. Tom Ford, with instantaneous caution, had already thrown himself clear and was out of the way.

It was well he did. Otherwise, he would have been splattered with brains and bits of skull, as Rae's bullet blew off the top of Boots Hobbs' head.

The booted gunman's own weapon exploded once more, but it was triggered only by the convulsion of his hand. The shot went wild, ricocheting off the stove and burying itself in a log wall. Then Hobbs' body was crumpling to the floor under the table and it was all over and Rae, who had landed on the floor himself with the thrust of his jump, was scrambling to his feet, gun still ready and cocked, breath coming hard, in sharp, audible pants.

Tom Ford came away from the wall against which he had thrown himself. His thin face was totally without expression. He looked down at Hobbs' body. Then he looked at his men.

"All right," he said harshly. "Somebody git a mop and a bucket and clean up this mess." Then he turned to Rae.

"You're a good man with an iron," he said. There was admiration in his voice.

Rae did not answer. He was gulping down the nausea of reaction.

Ford smiled thinly. "You can finish your drink now," he said, holding out Rae's glass. Rae took it with a hand that, he was surprised to see, did not shake. The whiskey tasted good; it helped a lot. He slid his Colt back into its holster.

He handed the glass back to Ford. Ford took it and also took the bottle that still sat upon the table.

"Come on," he said. "Let's get outta the way and let 'em clean up." There was discernible respect in his voice now. "I like the way you handle yourself when the chips are down. Crystal said you were a good man to work with; I believe her now. You and I have got some serious business to talk over. I never heard of a man rustlin' his own stock before, but nobody can say about Tom Ford that he don't like to try somethin' new when he gets th' chance. . . ."

V

Two days later, Rae Marsh saw before him once again the decaying log fort and scattered buildings of Bent's Crossing. He had ridden carefully, warily, back through Fletcher's Hole, taking time to learn more about the terrain, memorizing the run of streams, the hills and canyons and gulches of the place. It was necessary that he know the ground well: it was going to be his battlefield.

There was no doubt about that now, he thought, looking down at the town. With Tom Ford behind him—and he did not discount Crystal, either—he had his army, and the war could begin.

The way Rae had handled the fight with Boots Hobbs had been the credentials Ford had been waiting for. He was a man who respected strength, nerve, gunspeed. He was also, Rae had learned, in his own way a level-headed, cold-blooded businessman. He was chary about making a deal, tough about terms. But he had the organization—the guns, the way-stations at which rustled cattle could be held until blotted brands had healed, the buyers—and there was no way Rae could do without him.

And now the next move was— Well, he would consult with Crystal about that. In the meantime, he'd had a long ride; he was dirty, tired and hungry. He jigged the bay with spurs and set it at a high lope into town.

As its hoofs thudded on the hard-packed dirt of the main street, he was aware of eyes on him. Cleve Anders had done a good job of spreading the word about him. Well, the hell with Anders, too; Rae Marsh had his warpaint on today.

He pulled up in front of Crystal's place and swung down. The bay snorted and tugged its head toward a nearby watering trough, and before Rae tethered it, he led it to drink. While the animal dipped its muzzle in the water, he stood alertly, his eyes sweeping the street.

They were all watching him, the people of Bent's Crossing, all staring at him as if he were some sort of freak. He grinned wryly and deliberately let one hand swing near his gun butt, staring at a group of busybodies directly across the way. Immediately the knot of loafers broke up, faded back, intimidated. Marsh chuckled softly; but there was no mirth in the sound, and a nagging sense of danger kept his muscles taut. It was that sixth sense that made him turn and look in the other direction before he led the bay back to the hitchrack. And he was not even surprised; it was as if he had expected to see two figures clumping down the board sidewalk toward him, two men whom he recognized immediately—Cleve Anders and his own half brother, Will Marsh.

They were a hundred feet away and coming steadily, purposefully. Rae let the bay's reins drop; it would stand groundhitched. Then he moved clear of the watering trough and faced them.

As they approached, he could hear Will Marsh's

voice, low but excited. "Now, listen, Cleve," the kid was saying. "There ought to be a way to settle—"

"Shut up," Anders said. Then he stepped down off the sidewalk and into the street. Rae felt a peculiar kind of aliveness in his right arm and hand. I could kill him now, he thought. I could kill him and then I'd be clear of all this. But the thought went as quickly as it had come. Anders would have to draw first, and even if Rae beat him, there would still be Will. Suppose he drew, too? Something in Rae rebelled at the thought of facing the boy over the muzzle of a gun. It was not that he couldn't beat Will, but this was his own father's son, his own flesh and blood. . . .

So Rae slowly raised his right hand well away from the gun and stood spraddle-legged, with arms folded, waiting for them to come up.

As Anders covered the last few feet between them, he was grinning with that contemptuous twist of lips Rae had seen before, as if everyone but himself was dirt.

Anders stopped almost arm's length away, with Will behind him. "Well," he said. "You are the hard-haided one, ain't you?"

Rae said nothing. His eyes met those of Anders.

Anders did not flinch from his gaze. He said quietly, "I thought I told you to git the hell out of Fletcher's Hole. And to stay got."

"I'm particular about who I take orders from," Rae said.

Anders drew in a long breath. "Then it looks like you got to be taught another lesson, don't it?"

Rae's back was against his horse. He said, very softly, "You got another gunny sneaking up behind to hold the drop while you have your fun? It won't be so easy for him this time."

"There's nobody sneaking up," Will Marsh said shrilly. "What do you think we are?"

"I know about Anders," Rae said tersely. "I ain't made up my mind about you, yet."

"Don't take time to," Anders said. "Jest git on that horse and ride."

"Sorry," Rae said. "But I'm visitin' a friend here. So I guess I'll stick around."

Anders' eyes narrowed. "Hombre," he grated, "we've talked long enough. A little gun-whippin'—!" And his hand shot downward.

Rae did not even try to draw. But his body hurtled forward like an uncoiling spring. As Anders tried to pull out the gun, he locked his arms around Anders' body, pinioned him. His weight bore Anders rocking backwards. Anders tripped on the edge of the sidewalk; and the two of them crashed down onto the boards, Anders beneath, Rae on top. In that instant, Rae caught a glimpse of Will Marsh standing indecisively, hands spread. "Stay out of this!" he bawled desperately, and then his left hand locked on Anders' right wrist, as the big man tried to finish dragging his weapon from the holster.

They rolled there on the boards for a moment, then, fighting for the gun. Anders was strong as a bear; Marsh was a cougar of a man, whipcord tough, wiry. They rolled over and over along the sidewalk and all the strength years of hard range work had built into Rae's arm and wrist and hand went into the squeezing pressure he applied. Anders' gun went off once, firing skyward, and then, as Rae felt the bones of Anders' wrist shift beneath his grasp, Anders dropped the Colt.

Something leaped in Rae as he saw a boot-toe—
Will Marsh's toe—kick the gun and send it skittering out of reach down the sidewalk. Rae pulled
loose from Anders' grip, lurched panting to his
feet, backed into the middle of the street. "All
right," he heard himself rasp, and there was no
thought of his own gun. There was just the insane
desire in him to use his fists to deal out to Anders
what the other had dealt to him. He wanted to
beat Anders, hammer him, drive him
down. . . ."All right. Now, come on. Now. I won't
draw." Hardly realizing what he was doing, he
yanked the goldplated Colt and in a single motion
flipped it toward Will Marsh. "Hold that. Come
on, damn you, Anders. . . ."

Anders scrabbled to his feet, rubbing his wrist.
He looked sideways at his step-brother. "All right,
Will, you've got his gun—"

The boy looked from Anders to Rae. His thin
face was dead white, but there was color over his
cheekbones. "Maybe you'd better see what you can
do all by yourself, Cleve."

Anders sucked in a long breath. For an instant,
his face was furious. Then it broke into a wolfish
grin. "Maybe," he said, "you're right!" And he
threw himself at Rae Marsh, fists clubbed.

Marsh was waiting for him, feet planted. He
ducked low; Anders' first punch slammed into his
shoulder. It had enormous force, but he was braced
for it, and he was throwing one of his own. It went
under the big man's guard, caught him hard-on in
the belly. Rae heard Anders' breath whoosh by his
ear. He struck again.

Then he stepped back, his whole right side numb

from the force of Anders' blow. For a clocktick, they faced each other, both more wary now, appraising. Then Rae took the offensive, moved in quickly, tigerishly.

Anders was a fighter, and Anders hurt him. Anders rocked him with a right and a left, but Rae was dealing out punishment of his own, and that was all he cared about. He was not worried about Anders hurting him—not so long as he could hurt Anders worse. Weaving, snakelike, he bore in under the barrage of blows, his own arms hammering mercilessly, pounding Anders in gut and chest and face. Anders stepped back, gave ground, and Rae bore in harder.

But Anders grappled him this time, and in that bear hug Rae was bent back until at last he had to kick his feet out to keep his spine from snapping. He hit the ground hard, with breath-jarring impact and Anders on top of him, one hand on his throat, a thumb reaching for his eyes.

There was no time to recover his breath. Rae put every ounce of muscle into a pitching twist as wild as any outlaw horse could muster, felt Anders' weight shift, unseat. Then they were both rolling over and over in the dust, and there was no more give or take of fists; this was a savage, dirty battle for survival.

Cleve Anders had the size, but Rae Marsh had one crucial advantage. He'd been living a wolf's life for so long that he was hardened, he had endurance. And Anders, top dog of Fletcher's Hole, had taken it too easy in his royal role. His wind gave out while Rae's was still strong; his muscles went lax while there was iron left in Marsh's.

Rae felt that yielding, put everything he had into

one final surge. Then he was on top of Anders, pinning him, and there was red mist swimming before his eyes; he knotted his hand in the shag of Anders' hair, began slamming the man's head against the hardpacked dirt. "Boot me," he heard himself snarl, and it did not sound like his own voice at all. "Boot me and run me off my own range—"

Probably he would have killed Anders then and there, if a voice hadn't finally cleft through the fury that blotted out reason. "Rae! Rae, quit!" And then, "Will—you, somebody, drag him off!" Hands were clawing at him. He rose, turning, ready to club the owner of those hands, but then he found himself looking into Crystal's wide-eyed but determined face.

And Will Marsh was dragging at him, too, jerking him to his feet. He came fully erect, shook off all those hands, stepped away. He looked down at Anders, sprawled on the dirt. The man was out cold, a trickle of blood running from each nostril.

"Rae!" Crystal was saying over and over again —"Rae, Rae, come out of it!"

Rae shook his head, dragged a dusty sleeve across his face. Crystal was dabbing at the blood on his chin with a bit of white lace. "Are you all right?" she whispered. He could smell the fragrance of her perfume through the dust and blood that clogged his nostrils.

"I'm all right," he grated. He looked at Will Marsh. The boy stood there over the body of his step-brother, staring at Rae Marsh in awe. Rae walked toward him unsteadily and held out a hand. "I'll take my gun now," he said harshly.

For a moment the eyes of the half brothers met. Rae would have given a lot, then, to have been able to read what was in Will's gaze, but he could not. Wordlessly, the boy drew the golden gun from his waistband and thrust its butt toward Rae. Rae took it and eased it into his holster. Their eyes stayed locked for a second longer; then Will Marsh spun away and bent over Cleve Anders.

Crystal's fingers dug into Rae's arm. "Come on," she said urgently. "We've got to get you upstairs and patched up."

"So that's the deal," he told Crystal later. He had washed and she had patched his splits and bruises with arnica and courtplaster, and though he ached in every muscle he would be all right with rest. Just now, he had finished putting away a monstrous steak and a heap of fried potatoes and he was drinking scalding black coffee. "Thanks to you, I've got Tom Ford with me now."

"I hope you're still saying thanks later on," Crystal murmured. She sat across from him; and he thought he had never seen anything lovelier than the way she looked in her white summer dress. All this had just about been worth it just to meet somebody like her, he thought.

"What do you mean?" he asked as the import of her words sank in.

"Nothing," she said. "I just had some second thoughts later about sending you to Ford. It might have been a mistake; I don't know. But he was the only help I could think of."

"We'll make do with him," Rae said. "I think I know what you mean, though. He's a tough one. And with a mind of his own. But I think that as long as his interests are our interests, we can depend on him."

He set down the coffee cup. "Anyway, we're between a rock and a hard place. Where else can we turn but to Ford? He's got the men and the setup we need . . . and I've got to have the money from my share of those cattle if I ever hope to fight Anders in court and get clear title to my third of the place." He reached for his cigarette makings. "I can take a third of the beef, one way or the other. But I can't make off with a third of the range. Court is the only way I'll ever get that."

"You'd have got a hanging if you'd kept on banging Anders' head against the ground," Crystal said.

"I appreciate your pulling me off of him," Rae said. "If you hadn't, Will would have had to move in, and then it would have been me against Will. I wouldn't have wanted that."

"That's what I meant," she said. "Will couldn't just stand by and see you kill Cleve. You'd have had to take him on, too, and you'd have killed him and then they'd have hanged you."

Looking at her through cigarette smoke, he said, "You sound kind of like it might upset you for that to happen."

She did not answer. Rae went on quickly, "But it might have saved a lot of trouble in another way if you hadn't stopped me. When Anders gets wise to the fact that he's losing cattle, Ford thinks he'll hire on gunhands and there'll be killing anyway." He stood up. "I don't much like the thought of that. I've just come through one fight down in Lincoln County and—Dammit, of all the people in the world I had to find ruling the Circle M roost when I came here, why did it have to be Anders?"

He broke off as the corridor door opened and

Crystal's sister, Hallie, came in. She stood there shyly, her face a little flushed. "There's a . . . a man out here who wants to see Mr. Marsh," Hallie said.

Rae's hand instinctively dropped toward his hip. "Who is it?"

"Will Marsh," Hallie said.

Rae and Crystal looked at each other quickly, blankly, and then Rae strode to the door, gently pushing Hallie aside. He opened the door. Will stood there, thumbs hooked in belt. He removed them quickly as the door swung open. He looked past Rae to Crystal and Hallie and seemed faintly embarrassed.

"I want to see you for a minute," he said softly to Rae.

"Then come in," Rae said, standing aside.

Will entered hesitantly, removing his hat. He bowed slightly to Crystal and then to Hallie. "Mrs. Crystal. Miss . . ."

"Blaine," Crystal said. "Her name's Hallie Blaine. I was a Blaine before I married, and she's my sister."

"Miss Blaine," Will said. Rae noticed that his eyes lingered on Hallie's face for a moment; she flushed beneath his gaze and said something inaudible.

Then Will turned toward Rae. "You doggone near killed Cleve this morning," he said, and the softness had gone out of his voice.

"He asked for it," Rae said.

"I'm not saying he didn't," Will said. "I had to send him back to the outfit in a buckboard; he was too banged up to ride."

There was a moment of silence then. Rae said,

presently, his voice tense: "Well? You here to take up the fight?"

The boy shook his head slowly. "No. I came to tell you that you ain't got a Chinaman's chance if you hang on around here any longer. Cleve's swearing to kill you on sight now, and he means what he says. He'll do it if he has to hire half a dozen gunslingers to get it done."

"And you?" Rae was still tense.

"Me?" Will's voice faltered for a moment. In that instant, he looked very young, despite the guns on his hips. "Me? I—" He spread his hands. "What can I do? I think that letter you had was straight. I think we're brothers. But Cleve's my brother, too—I was raised up with him. If he says . . . if he says no, I can't make him say yes." He broke off; his face changed. "I wish you'd go away," he said. "I wish you'd go away and not crowd us. Maybe with you gone I could talk Cleve into—"

"You couldn't talk Cleve into anything," Crystal said harshly.

Will hesitated. Then he said, "No, I reckon not. I reckon nobody could." His hand moved; only then did Rae notice that Will had a third gun stuck in his waistband, and he recognized it immediately. Will took it out and held it toward Rae.

"I guess the only real reason I had for coming was to give this back to you," he said. "It's the one we took off you out at Circle M."

Rae took it slowly, looking his half brother in the eyes. "Thanks." He turned to Crystal, fishing the goldplated gun from its holster. "I guess you can have this back now."

She looked at him strangely. "Maybe you'd like to keep it a while longer."

Rae thought a second. Then he said, "I can always use an extra iron." He dropped the golden gun back into its scabbard and thrust his own into his waistband. Turning back to Will, he said, "I'd like to talk to you a little more. In private. If you got the time."

Crystal arose, touching her sister's elbow. Hallie had been standing there staring at Will Marsh; she came alive with a start. "We've got things we can do in the other room," Crystal said.

When the women had gone, Rae motioned to a chair. "Sit down. Cuppa coffee?"

Will shook his head, as he dropped into a chair. Rae looked at him a moment. Then he said, "That's a lot of iron you're packing. Two guns. About twice as much as most folks get along with."

Will's face came suddenly, boyishly, alive. "I can use 'em both, too. I've practiced. I can draw as fast lefthanded as I can with my right."

"So what?" Rae said.

"Huh?" Will looked at him blankly.

"I said, so what? Don't you know if you pack that kind of hardware around, sooner or later somebody's going to make you use it?"

"I hope they do," Will said. "I'd like to see anybody get the drop on me." He rocked forward in his chair excitedly. "I'll bet not even the Kid could do it. Look, you know the Kid. Bonney. Is he really as fast as they say?"

Something in Rae curled up sickly at Will's glittering eyes, the look of obsession that came over his face. It was a look he knew—he'd seen the same look on a buck-toothed face not much older than

Will's, the face of another man completely obsessed with guns, the face of a man who sooner or later was bound to die by gunfire.

"He's fast," Rae said coldly. "But he's also a cowardly little back-shooter when he gets the chance."

"I don't believe that about him," Will said quickly.

"I know him," Rae said. "I fought alongside him, till I got a belly-full of him. Dammit, why don't you leave those guns at home and forget about 'em? In another ten years maybe things will be so nobody will have to pack a gun no more. In the meantime, you don't want to—"

Will stood up, face flushed. "I want people to know my name," he said angrily. "Like they know Bonney's." He paused. "Like they know yours," he finished.

"They don't know mine," Rae said quickly.

"You think not? I've done some inquiring around. You're known. A top gunhand, everybody says. And yet you stand there lecturing me—"

Rae saw he was getting nowhere. He waved a hand wearily. "All right. Kill your own snakes. I just hope one of 'em don't kill you." His voice changed. "I want you to do me a favor."

"What?"

"I want you to tell me," Rae said softly, "all about how John Marsh died."

A shadow, pain-filled, crossed Will's face. "Don't make me talk about that," he said. "It wasn't . . . pretty."

"I want to hear about it," Rae said. "I've got to hear about it."

Will hesitated, gnawing his lower lip. Then he

looked down at the floor. "They call it cancer," he said. "It gets started inside you and it eats you up."

"I know what it does," Rae said. "Go on."

"He got to feeling bad. He went to Chicago for an examination. They tried to make him stay there, but he wouldn't. He came home, said by God he was going to die on his own home range. He was a tough old man."

"Yeah," Rae said.

"So damned tough," Will went on, "that for awhile we thought he was whipping it. Hell, even the doctor was surprised. Why, just the day before he died, the doctor said he ought to last for sixty days longer, anyhow."

"Was he doped up?" Rae asked.

"A good part of the time," Will said. "That stuff hurts."

"Yeah," Rae said. He thought of the old man dying in agony, waiting for him. Sixty days longer . . . and then dead. "Did he ever say anything about me?"

Will hesitated. "Maybe so, maybe no."

"What do you mean?"

"I mean, he said a couple of times there was something he was waiting for before he died. Then . . ." Will's voice trembled. "Then . . . the day before it happened, he was about half under the dope, half out of it. . . . Cleve and I was there. He got to talking about . . . about our brother. About how our brother we had never seen was coming soon. And that we had to . . . treat him right . . . treat him like a brother . . ."

"Did he tell you any more? About how I come to be separated from him?"

"No, only that, that I heard. He was giving out

then. Cleve bent over him, says, 'Dad, what's that? What do you mean?' And he whispered something to Cleve, but I didn't git it. I asked Cleve later, but he said it was nothing; just the dope talking. Anyhow . . . next morning we come in his room and found him dead. The doctor said it wasn't even the cancer—that to take him off that quick, it must have been his heart, failing under the strain."

"I see," Rae murmured, feeling oddly cold, his mind reaching for something it could not quite grasp, not quite believe.

"And then a few days later you show up," Will said. He put on his hat. "I wish . . . really, maybe if you'd go away, there'd be a way to work this out."

"We'll work it out while I'm here," Rae said harshly.

"What do you aim to do?"

"Nothing that's going to hurt you," Rae said. "But I aim to have what's coming to me. What my father wanted me to have."

"Uh-huh. Well—" Will started toward the door.

"Wait," Rae said.

Will turned.

"You stand clear of it," Rae said. "For God's sake, will you do that? Take off those two damned guns and stand clear?"

Will just looked at him a moment. "I don't know what I'm gonna do yet," he said. "But I told you—Cleve's my brother, too." Then he turned and went out.

VI

DURING THE next few days, Rae Marsh skulked the Circle M range like a lobo wolf. More than once he held his horse's muzzle to keep it from nickering when a Circle M rider passed by as he and his mount hid from view. It was a furtive, tense mission that he had sent himself upon—nothing less than to make a rough range tally of Circle M stock. He wanted his third, no more, no less, and his third would come, he reckoned after he had made his survey, to the staggering total of a thousand head of stock. That was a lot of beef to rustle. It was hardly likely that Ford, no matter how good he was at his trade, would be able to lift more than a couple of hundred head before Cleve Anders got wise to what was going on. And when he did, he'd have Circle M swarming with gunhung guards. Rae's spirits sank as he thought of all the trouble, the warfare, that lay ahead.

He was thinking of that, contemplating it gloomily, while he waited in darkness for Tom Ford at their appointed place of rendezvous. This was a narrow canyon in the tangled country at the very edge of Circle M, where its range butted against the badlands. A small bunch of prime beeves had worked its way in this direction, and Rae had chosen it for their first target, figuring that if it were missed at all, Circle M would assume that the cattle had grazed on into the rough country.

Rae had led a tough life, and he had been down some strange paths in his time, but this was his first essay at rustling. He realized that, ironically enough, it was a trade like any other, and there was a great deal he didn't know about it. He would have to leave all the "business" details to Ford, the expert. He did not like having to surrender even that much control over this operation, but there was no way around it.

He was sitting on a rock in a puddle of shadow when his horse, whose reins he held in his hand, jerked its head up. Rae arose silently and ran his hand up the horse's neck, checked the direction of the cocked ears. Just in time, he got his fingers over the animal's muzzle, pinching tight the nostrils, or the bay would have whickered.

But the pointed ears were pointed in the right direction. That should be Ford coming.

Rae waited tensely. Presently he could hear what the horse had heard far earlier—the click of iron-shod hooves on rocks. Then, ghostlike, figures materialized in the darkness up-canyon. Rae dropped one hand to his gun. "Ford?" His voice was soft.

There was an interval between question and answer. Then Ford's voice said, in a normal tone, "That you, Marsh?"

Rae relaxed. "It's me." He led the horse out of shadow.

Ford had ten riders at his back. As Rae swung up into the saddle and drew alongside, Ford said, "Where's the bunch?"

"Out of this canyon and across the ridge. There's a little valley on the ridge's yon side. About forty head there, all prime."

"Forty head?" Ford sounded incredulous. "That all?"

"That's a lot of beef."

Ford snorted. "I'm set up to operate, man. I can lift a hundred and fifty head and fight while we're doing it, if I have to. Forty head . . . that's a lot of risk for not much return."

"No risk," Rae said. "I've been watching most of the day. Not a rider in sight."

Ford was silent for a moment. "All right," he said at last. "We'll see." He reined in. "Put the bags on 'em," he said, turning, passing the word. Then he swung down. Rae watched in astonishment, and with some admiration, as each rider muffled all four hooves of his mount with leather shoes that tied around the fetlocks. Only then did he realize how silently the riders had come. Looking at Ford's mount, he saw that bit chains had been done away with, all leather oiled to cut squeaking to a maximum, that Ford—and, he supposed, all the others—wore cavalry spurs, without rowels, to eliminate even that much jingling and clinking.

Ford passed him similar leather bags. "I brought some for you," he said, and Rae put them on the bay, which stood patiently, only snorting a little at this novelty.

"You've got this thing down to a science," Rae said softly, when they had all remounted.

"I don't do it for fun," Ford said. "Okay, lead on." With Rae at their head, the dozen men moved forward through the night like ghosts.

As Rae had known they would be, the cattle were bedded in the valley. Ford halted on the ridge above, sent his men out like a general dispersing troops. First the guards went out wide, in a semicircle. Then, within their protection, the rustlers rode down to rouse the herd and get it moving.

They did it, Rae saw, with the precision and touch of master cowmen. There was not a one of them who would not have made a top hand on any spread. Ford himself was everywhere, almost exactly like a trail boss on a cattle drive, or a round-up boss. Out to make certain the guards were alert, checking point, swing, flanks and making sure the drag didn't linger. There was nothing for Rae to do but keep clear of the operation.

Riders and horses alike seemed to have cat's eyes, to be able to see in the moonless dark. In an incredibly swift passage of time, the cattle were being pinched into the narrow canyon and headed toward the breaks. Rae followed the drag, along with Ford and a rearguard whose hands never left their guns.

When the herd was through that narrow canyon and traversing a large one into which it branched, Ford seemed to relax. "All right," he said. "I guess we're in the clear." His voice held grudging admiration. "That was good spotting."

"Thanks," Rae said dryly.

"It'll be awhile before we have any money for these," Ford said. "My buyers won't take 'em unless the brands are healed."

"All right," Rae said.

"But that doesn't mean we stop until then," Ford said. "Forty head's nothing. I can handle three hundred, four hundred, keep 'em moving right along. You find us another bunch. Something with a tally up around a hundred."

"A bunch that size'll be pretty close in," Rae said.

"I don't care if it's close in or not," Ford said. "We have to move fast. I want to get as much as we can before Anders can get wise and bring in enough men to give us trouble. It's one thing to come up against cowpunchers when you're making a lift, but it's another to come up against gun-hands."

Something in Ford's voice sent a chill prickling down Rae's spine. God help the cowpuncher, it seemed to imply, who got in Ford's way. Suddenly Rae was aware of a sickness within him, a disgust with himself and this whole operation. And yet, he was in too deep now to get out; there was nothing to do but play it through to the end.

Ford misread his silence. "You don't have to worry. You'll get your cut of the money all right when it comes in. I told you, I'm a businessman. I play it straight with my partners."

"Sure," Rae said.

"You get another bunch spotted, you leave a note in the same place and meet up. We'll be along."

"Sure," Rae said again.

"I've seen better," Ford said, "but it's been a good night's work. Like you said, they're all prime; they'll fetch a good price." He thrust out a hand. "Well, *adios*."

Rae took it. It was thin and bony and somehow repellent. *"Adios,"* he said. He was glad to rein the bay around and strike off through the darkness toward Bent's Crossing. He could not help but be nagged by the feeling that he was working for Ford as much as Ford was working for him.

He felt better when he could see Crystal again. She was waiting for him the next morning in her place. "Well?" she asked. Her face looked a little drawn, her eyes smudged with circles, as if she had not slept well.

Rae shut the door of her room behind him. "It went all right," he said. "We lifted forty head."

Crystal let out a long breath and sat down. "There wasn't any trouble?"

"None," Rae said. "We didn't see a soul." He stared at her. "What's the matter? We've made our first move against Cleve Anders and you look like the world's come to an end."

Crystal shook her head. "I'm sorry," she said. "I just—well, I didn't sleep last night. A lot of things could have happened."

"But nothing did," Rae grinned. A good night's sleep and the coming of dawn had lifted his spirits. He was beginning to feel exultant over their easy coup of the night before. If it just all went that well . . .

"Well," he went on, "ain't you even going to offer me breakfast?"

Crystal's dark brows raised. "You're beginning to feel right at home here, aren't you, mister?"

Rae's grin faded. "I can leave if you want me to."

"No," she said quickly. She made a gesture with her hand. "I'll have some food brought up for you. Hallie! Please—?"

When her sister had gone downstairs, Rae dropped into a chair and rolled a cigarette.

"You know," he said, "if I could get clear title to

my third of Circle M, you know what I'd do with it?"

"What?" Crystal seemed restless. She bustled about the table, clearing it for the breakfast that would be brought in.

"I'd call off my war with Anders, sell it back to him and Will for a reasonable price, and use the money from it to buy another spread somewhere else."

Crystal looked at him. "Where?"

"I know some pretty country down in northern New Mexico. Land's cheap now—it'll be higher once they get the Apaches herded in for good and all. And a man could bring up Mexican cattle and breed 'em up with a few good bulls and before long he could have himself a nice herd . . ."

Crystal's mouth seemed to harden. "You're spinning daydreams," she said tartly.

Rae nodded gravely. "I know. But I got to give myself some reason for doing all this. Besides just gettin' revenge on Anders. And tryin' to carry out a dead man's wishes." He stood up. Something was working inside him, something he did not quite want to put a name to yet. He walked to the window and looked out. "Someday this country'll tame down," he said. "There'll come a time when a man can walk down a street like that and not have to tote a gun to protect himself. This'll be good land, then. I'd like to have a piece of it. I've had my share of fightin', of carrying this damn' thing around with me." He put his hand on his gun. "I'm ready for a place like I was talking about." He turned, walked across the room to Crystal, and took her arm.

"I'm ready for a woman to share it with me,

too," he said, and he pulled her to him and kissed her.

For just a moment, her lips seemed to yield to his, her body to go pliant in his arms. Then, with surprising strength, she was pushing him away, and her voice was trembling with cold fury.

"Don't you ever try to do that to me again, mister, you understand me?" Her face was paper-white, her lips peeled back from white teeth, her eyes flashing.

Startled by her vehemence, Rae blinked. "Crystal," he said, groping for words. "Don't you understand what I was trying to say?"

Crystal drew in a breath that made her breasts rise under her tight bodice. "I understand this," she said in a low, intense voice. "I understand that I've had one man killed out here already, a man I loved shot down like a dog. I'm not . . . I'm not going to let myself in for anything like that again. Not ever, do you understand?" She was beautiful in her intensity, and something hurt inside Rae with the wanting of her. He took a step toward her, but she put out her hands. "No!" she flared. "I mean it. We'd better get this straight right now. We're in this together for one reason and one reason only. I've got a debt to settle with Cleve Anders and working together we can settle it. That's all you mean to me, you hear? Nothing else but that."

Rae stared at her for a moment. There was in him then an impulse to do one of two things—either take her in his arms despite her protests, or go through that door, close it behind him, and never come back, ride out of Fletcher's Hole altogether. He stifled both impulses. With all the will he could muster, he got control of himself.

"All right," he said coolly. "We'll play by your rules, then."

Crystal turned away. "That's right," she said. "We play by my rules. Now, sit down. Hallie will be here with your breakfast in a minute."

VII

THE MORE HE watched him in action, the more Rae had to acknowledge that Tom Ford was a master of his trade. Rae could understand now why cattlemen would spare no effort to stamp out even the most petty rustling. Once let it get organized the way Ford had it organized, and it could pick a range clean in fantastically short time.

For that was what Ford was doing to Circle M. With Rae acting as spotter and extra hand on the raids, Ford would swoop down on a herd and, with no waste motion, make it disappear almost as if by magic. Nor did Ford insist on confining his raids to night operations. As it began to become apparent to the Circle M that cattle were vanishing, their riders prowled at night, standing guard. Together, Ford and Rae evolved a technique for daytime raids, striking when least expected and when most Circle M riders were holed up sleeping off their previous sleepless night.

Once, in the most daring move of all, Rae himself infiltrated into the very heart of the Circle M home ranch under cover of darkness. With Ford and his men poised out on the range, Rae, silent, only a darker shadow in black night, touched a

match to one, two, three Circle M haystacks. As
the hay flared, lighting the night, triggering confusion, drawing in riders from the outlying range,
Ford hit, and another seventy head of Circle M
beef seemed to disappear into thin air.

Rae himself had a breathless time of it. The night
was alive with Circle M men. Yet somehow he
slithered his way clear, made it to freedom without
being challenged.

"You're good," Ford acknowledged after that.
"You're good and you're smart. I wish you was
working with me full time. Together we could
make ourselves a pile . . ."

Rae shook his head. "A thousand head," he said
tersely. "That's the maximum we lift from Circle
M, and we'll be lucky to get half that. But when
we've got all we can get without having to fight a
war, that's when we break it off. It's just been luck
we haven't got anybody killed so far—either on
our side or on Circle M's."

"Luck?" said Ford. "It ain't luck. Listen, I don't
want any killing any more than you do. It's bad for
business. Oh, if it comes to a fight, we're ready, but
I'd a lot rather keep on the way we're going, slick
and clean, than to have to shoot for my beef."

Rae was reassured by that. He had become
almost haunted by the fear that some night they
would run into a trap, that Circle M men against
whom he had no grudge, who were only doing their
work, fighting for their brand, would be slaughtered—and if they were, their blood would be on
his hands. Sooner or later, he thought sickly, it was
bound to happen. And what turned his blood cold
was the fear that in some such nocturnal battle he

might fire at some dark shape who would turn out
to be ... Will.

Rae pulled the mask up over his face.

Like the masks worn by all the other rustlers, it
was a black bandanna that left only his eyes unhid-
den. Day or night, Ford left nothing to chance; all
of his riders must go masked.

Ford's voice was low, muffled. "Everybody
ready?"

A murmur of assent came from his riders.

"Let's move in, then," Ford said.

It was a black-dark night, and this looked, Rae
thought, like the easiest raid so far. He had
watched the bunch of fifty cattle all day and had
seen no sign of a guard. Nor was the explanation
hard to guess; they were not prime stock, and Circle M had its hands full trying to keep an eye on its
better beef, held closer in. But the grass would not
support the whole Circle M run held in a close
area; only the cream of the herd could be guarded;
the culls had to graze out to relieve strain on the
grass and take their chances.

Now the ghost-file of riders threaded its way
down a draw, then fanned out on a flat. Ahead Rae
could see the dark blotches of sleeping cattle. Silently Ford's men went about their work. They got
the herd up, bunched, and moving into the draw,
traveling well. The night's march would take some
fat off of them, but Ford had ranches at his dis-
posal where they could graze it back on before they
were sold.

Rae dropped back to where Ford was urging on
his drag riders. "Everything quiet?"

"Seems to be," Ford grunted.

"This makes about two hundred fifty we've picked up so far, total, huh?"

"Closer to three hundred," Ford said. "But it's not gonna stay this easy, I'm afraid." He twisted in his saddle. "We've been mighty damned lucky so far. I've got a hunch—" He broke off.

"What's wrong?" Rae asked tensely.

"I don't know, yet," Ford muttered. "But something . . ." He jigged his horse and galloped up to the flank, with Rae alongside. "Curt," he said to the man there, "where's Doak and Joe?"

Curt twisted in his saddle. "Don't know. Was here a little while ago."

"Damn it," Ford grunted. With Rae alongside, he circled the herd. There was no sign of the missing men.

"There's something up," Ford said at last, reining in. "Doak and Joe both—they're old hands. They wouldn't have just blundered off and got themselves lost. They shoulda come in off of guard by now and joined the herd. I—"

He broke off, straightening in the saddle. A low whistle, a nightbird's call, came from the top of a nearby swell of ground. "That's them," Ford rapped. He jerked his horse around. The whistle came again, and he galloped toward it with Rae beside him.

"Here, boss," somebody said from darkness. Ford pulled up.

"Doak? Joe?"

"Right here." Figures moved against the darkness. "We caught ourselves somethin'."

Rae and Ford swung down. "What you got?" Ford asked.

"Circle M man," one of Ford's men said. "We were comin' in to catch up with the herd when we run into him. I 'tracted his attention, Joe jumped him from behind. Didn't want to use a gun."

"No," Ford said. "You got his mouth tied shut?"

"Gagged good," one said. "Both hands tied. We got his horse, too."

"Load him on it," Ford said. "Bring him along. Keep a sharp eye on him. Any more around?"

"Haven't seen none. And he swears he's the only one."

Ford cursed softly under his breath. "What's a lone man doin' blunderin' around the range at night? Bound to be more."

"With a cocked gun in his belly, he says not. He'd been in town to see a gal. Took on some liquor, stayed late. He was purty drunk when we nabbed him, but he sobered up in a hurry."

"Well, he'd better hope nobody jumps us. If they do, he'll be first to go. Bring him along and we'll take care of him later." Ford remounted.

As they headed back towards the herd, Rae said, "What do you aim to do with him?"

"Cut his throat," Ford said. "What else? A gun makes too much noise."

Rae pulled in his horse. "No," he said harshly.

Ford jerked up his own mount. "What?" His voice was full of astonishment. Then, before Rae could answer, he put the animal in motion again. "Come on, we'll talk it out later. Thing to do now is get these cattle away."

Two hours of hard pushing later, they were eight, ten miles off Circle M range, in one of a laby-

rinth of canyons. With three more hours to go to
dawn, there was ample getaway time for the herd,
but none to waste. There was rock and lava still to
cross, where the trail would fade out, baffling
pursuit.

Rae had ridden the whole time behind the two
men with the captive, watching them carefully. It
went against his grain enough to think of killing a
Circle M man in heated battle; the thought of
standing by to watch one murdered in cold blood
could not be borne. He did not know what he
would do when Ford finally decided the time had
come; but he knew that he could not stand by and
do nothing.

But he had no illusions. Ford had already said it
to him, as they entered the badlands. "Hell, business is business. And in this business, you don't
leave nobody to talk. We'll hide his carcass where
not even the buzzards'll find it, and then nobody
will ever know what happened to him."

That had been when Rae had dropped back to
keep an eye on the captive and his captors.

Now Ford signaled for a halt. The herd was
milled and bunched in the confines of the canyon,
given time to blow. The two rustlers reined in, the
Circle M captive between them. In darkness and
with a gag in his mouth, Rae could not have recognized him even if he had seen him head on, which
there had been no opportunity to do. But as Ford
walked his horse up, he gave the command: "All
right. Somebody strike a light."

There was pungent sulphur smell and the flare of
a match. In its blooming light, which lasted only a
moment, Rae got a glimpse of a terrified face, eyes

bulging with fear above a bandanna used as a gag. Then darkness again; but he had recognized the man. Clyde: the one who had come up behind him with a gun that first day at Circle M, when Anders had hammered him into the ground.

"All right," Ford said. "Joe. You do it."

Every muscle, every nerve in Rae Marsh's body strung itself taut. "No," he said.

Ford sighed. "Hold it, Joe. All right. Come over here. Let's talk." They rode out of earshot of the prisoner.

"Listen, now," Ford said with savagery, reining in. "When we're making a lift like this, I'm the boss, you understand? These are my men, it's my outfits and contacts we use, we take the risks. So you call the tune on the big picture, but you leave details like this to me, you understand?"

"I understand this," Rae said evenly. "There'll be no murder done—not like this."

"Dammit," Ford said, his voice still savage, "that ranny knows how many we are; he knows which way this herd has gone . . ."

"I can't help that," Rae said.

"He may even have recognized us."

"Not with masks. Not in this dark."

"Listen," Ford said. "We can't take him with us. And if we turn him loose, he knows how we operate, which way we head—he knows too damned much. He'll have this range stirred up against us like a hornet's nest."

"It'll be stirred up anyhow," Rae said. "Crystal's word is that Anders is combin' the whole state for gunslingers. He's buildin' an army anyhow."

"No point, then, in givin' him any more information than he's already got to help him use it against us."

"I can't help it," Rae said. "You're not gonna slit his throat like a shoat at hog-killin' time and leave him for the buzzards. I won't stand for that."

"What are you gonna do about it?" Now Ford's voice was sardonic.

Rae drew in a long breath. His voice was very cold, very hard. "I'll decide that if you crowd me."

Ford was silent for a moment. Then he rasped, "Maybe I misjudged you. I thought from the way you handled Boots Hobbs—"

"It's one thing to down a man when he's comin' against you. It's another thing to cut his throat in cold blood."

Ford was silent for a minute or two. He moved his horse and Rae tensed; he and Ford were knee to knee now, facing each other. Rae's hand flexed. He did not want to fight Ford and his men for the life of that captive, but it was beginning to look as if there were no other way out. Ten against one— long odds, he thought bitterly. But Ford would be the first to go. . . .

Almost as if Ford could read his mind, the rustler said, finally, "All right, dammit." His horse clattered across the rocks. His muffled voice rang out, sharp with anger. "Let him go."

There were angry protests; Ford beat them down harshly. "I said let him go." His voice lanced at the captive. *"Hombre,* you're gittin' off light this time. But you run your mouth, it won't be so light. If I was you, I wouldn't even go back to Circle M. I'd keep on ridin' until I was so far away from

Fletcher's Hole the mail couldn't reach me. You *sabe?"*

The man gave a muffled grunt.

Ford said: "Untie his hands."

Then Rae, tensely watchful, fingers still poised by the stock of his Colt, heard the slap of a quirt on a horse's rump. "Hyahh!" somebody barked; and the animal's shoes clicked on stone as it galloped back down the canyon.

Ford came back to where Rae was sitting. "Satisfied?"

"I reckon," Rae said. "Thanks."

"You won't thank me when we've got an army to fight," Ford said. "You headed back to Bent's Crossing?"

"The wide way around," Rae said.

"Okay. Keep in touch." Ford turned his horse. "All right," he barked. "Line 'em out!" Rae held in the bay, as the herd got under way. Then he turned it, swung into a side canyon, and began the long, circuitous ride back to town.

VIII

DAWN was streaking the sky when Rae Marsh swung down off the weary bay in the cover of the great shadow cast by the decaying log fort outside Bent's Crossing. Usually, after a night of raiding with Ford, he managed to make it back to the town itself before daylight, to ease into Crystal's place and to bed down in the tiny closet of a room upstairs that she had allocated to his use. But he was running late this time; the argument about the captive had held him up, and he did not dare be seen riding into Bent's Crossing on a hard-traveled horse, obviously having been up all the night himself—not after the released captive might have pinpointed to Anders exactly when and how this latest cattle-theft had taken place.

But the old fort offered cover and a chance to catch forty winks. He had watered the bay at the last stream, and it would have to do without fodder until he put it in the livery stable later in the day. There were a few rotting boxstalls in the fort; he hid the bay in one of those and found a crevice behind some fallen roof joists where he could roll up in his blanket and get some sleep.

But, tired as he was, sleep was a long time coming tonight. This whole deal was souring more and more. Three hundred head, he thought as he lay there; his half of that should be enough to get court action started. And if they kept up, if they tried to rustle the entire fantastic third, a thousand cattle, somebody innocent was going to get killed in the process. He did not care about Ford's men; he did not care about Anders or any professional gunmen Anders might hire; he did not even care about himself. But he cared about the ordinary Circle M riders who were only doing their duty to their brand—and most of all, he cared about Will. Sooner or later, if there was fighting, Will was bound to be sucked into it.

Maybe the best thing to do, the smart thing, the sensible one, would be to call off Ford. The cattle thief had made a good haul and he was smart enough to understand that their luck had been pushed about as far as it would go.

Well, he would think about it in the morning. Right now, he had to have some shuteye. He rolled over, pulled the blanket up around his ears, put his hat over his eyes, and with his head on the seat of his saddle, finally dropped into exhausted, dreamless sleep.

Daylight awakened him, lancing through gaps in the tumbled down roof above him. He sat up, as instantly alert as a waking wolf, head swiveling, hand reaching for gun, but all was still. He could hear the bay stamping in the stall, even hear the rumbling of its empty belly. Rae relaxed and slowly got to his feet, brushing chips of rotten wood from shirt and chaps.

There was a brush and curry comb in his bag of

possibles, and he used them to brush the crusted foam and curled hair of a hard night's travel off the bay. Then, after making careful reconnaissance to make sure no one was around the fort to see him emerge, he saddled the bay, tied his blanket roll behind, and loped across the flat toward the town.

Boldly, as if he'd been out for a morning's ride, he rode down the town's main street. The bay needed feeding, but first he had to get his signals straight with Crystal. She was his alibi, she and Hallie.

The younger sister, who had no idea what was going on, had been confused and reluctant at first, but she depended on Crystal and had to trust her. Along with a few of Crystal's most trusted employees, she would swear, if necessary, that Rae had been at Crystal's place all night. So far it had not been necessary for either Crystal or Hallie to perjure themselves on Rae's behalf; there was no scrap of evidence to link him with the rustling, and Anders had stayed well away from Rae. But Rae did not fool himself that the beating he had given Anders had hammered fear into the man; Anders was only biding his time.

In the meanwhile, Rae got a certain heady pleasure out of openly defying Anders in front of the town, of exhibiting himself as proof that here, at least, was one man who refused to dance when Anders called the tune. In a way, it was as much a method of striking against Anders as the rustling; it undermined the respect, awe, and fear in which he was held by the townspeople.

The swinging doors of Crystal's place closed behind his back. It was late enough now so that customers were in here and Crystal had come downstairs; decorous in a high-necked black dress, she moved from table to table, greeting, laughing, joking. When she happened to look up and saw Rae Marsh crossing the room, she put one hand to her breast quickly, then dropped it. As soon as she could, without seeming hasty, she came to where he had sat down at a vacant able.

"Whiskey?" the man from behind the bar asked, as she came up. Rae shook his head.

"No," he said. "Coffee." The man nodded and turned away. Crystal sat down across from him. Her face was very white.

"How did it go?" she asked tautly.

"All right, I guess," Rae said.

"There wasn't any trouble?"

"No. None to speak of." He frowned. "What's the matter with you?"

"Anders is in town. Over at the marshal's office."

Rae leaned back in the chair, took out his makings. "I don't know that that's got anything to do with me. I was here all night, wasn't I?"

"Yes," Crystal said. "Of course. Only I—I don't like it."

"If they got no evidence," Rae said, "they can't arrest me."

"You don't know Anders and the marshal." Her index and middle finger linked themselves together. "They're like that."

"I don't care what they're like," Rae said. "Far as they're concerned, I'm clean." He leaned forward. "As long as you stand by me."

"You know I'll stand by you," Crystal said. There was an odd tremor in her voice. "All the same, it might be a good idea if you—"

"Run? Once I start that, I'll have to keep it up." Rae waited until the barman had set down the coffee and moved off. Crystal poured a cup and pushed it toward him. "Anyway, I've been thinking—"

"Thinking what?"

"Thinking that maybe I'm far enough along so I can go to court. That maybe—"

Boots on the sidewalk outside, the boots of several men, interrupted him. He turned quickly, hand sliding under the table where it could get to his gun if need be. The batwing doors vibrated behind Anders and a lanky man with a star on his vest and two other punchers behind them—and, at the very tail end of the procession, Will Marsh.

They stood there for a second or two, eyes sweeping the room as all sound in it died. Then, spotting Rae, they came toward him slowly, carefully, the rawboned marshal, a man of about forty, in front.

Anders stayed beside the marshal. The others, including Will, fanned out into a semi-circle.

Rae looked up at them coolly.

"All right, gentlemen," he said softly. "What is it?"

The marshal had a hoarse, braying voice. "Rae Marsh, you're under arrest."

"If you're smart," Anders added, "you'll come peaceable." His mouth quirked wolfishly. "If you ain't smart, we'll take you out feet first."

Rae kept his temper in check. His eyes went from the marshal to Anders and back again. "Under arrest," he said. "Well, well. Any particular charges?"

"There're charges," Anders said.

"Let the lawman talk," Rae snapped.

"The charge is murder," the marshal said.

Crystal let out a gasp. Rae felt his own blood seem to freeze. But he kept his voice steady, even. "Murder? What're you talking about? I ain't killed anybody. Who's been murdered?"

"One of my hands," Anders said. "A feller named Clyde Brennan. Bushwhacked. He must have been dropped by rustlers that run off some more of my beef last night. We found him out on the edge of my north range this mornin'. Buzzards led us to him."

"Clyde Brennan," Rae said. His brain was racing, even as his stomach knotted sickly. "That would be the hombre held the gun on me the day you tried to stomp me into the dirt."

"Brennan disarmed you when you tried to shoot me," Anders said coolly. "Yes. He's the man. And you never forgot your grudge against him, did you?"

"Brennan's dead?" Rae was still fighting for time.

"As a doornail."

Clyde Brennan. Last night's prisoner. The one Rae had striven to save, risked his own life for. And . . . *he double-crossed me,* Rae thought. *Damn him. Damn Ford.*

It was plain to him what had happened now. As soon as Rae had left Ford's outfit and was away from the herd, Ford had sent a man after Brennan. *Dead men can't shoot off their mouths. . . .*

Rae licked his lips. "I didn't kill Clyde Brennan," he said. "I haven't killed anybody . . . on this range."

Crystal's voice was surprisingly clear, steady. "You say Brennan was killed last night?"

"By the signs of it," Will Marsh said. He moved forward a little, hands hooked in his criss-crossed shell belts.

"Then Rae Marsh couldn't have done it," Crystal said coolly.

"Why not, ma'am?" The marshal's voice was respectful enough.

"Because," Crystal said, "because he was . . . upstairs all last night."

"He's got a room up there?"

"Yes," Crystal said. Her face was pale, a spot of color on each cheekbone.

"A man can go into a room and come out again," Anders sneered. "You don't know he was in his room."

Crystal drew in a deep breath. "He wasn't in *his* room," she said.

Rae looked at her, startled. She was crucifying herself, smearing her reputation before all the town, with this lie designed to save him. And she . . . she didn't even truly know whether he had killed Clyde Brennan or not. For all she knew, he might be guilty of the murder. Yet she would still go this far to save him. . . . Something clenched inside Rae. "Crystal—" he began.

"It's the truth," Crystal said. "I'll swear to it."

"Hush," Rae said. "Hush, Crystal." He took his right hand from under the table, slowly, cautiously. With equal slowness, he got to his feet. His eyes swept over them for a long second before he spoke. "I'll tell you again. I didn't kill Clyde Brennan. You got a warrant?"

"Warrant," Anders jeered. "Who's going to ride

all the way to Grand River City to git a warrant? There ain't no judge in Bent's Crossin'."

"Then you're arrestin' me illegal. Suppose . . ." His hands were high, his voice cool. "Suppose I won't come in?"

"You'll come," Anders said, "or we'll take you. Eh, Will?"

Will Marsh stepped around to confront Rae. His thin face was white, his eyes feverish with excitement. He looked like a child playing with his father's guns, Rae thought. His voice shook with stress; Rae saw immediately that Anders had been working on him all morning.

"You'll come," Will parroted his step-brother. "Don't you forget, I'm half owner of Circle M. Clyde Brennan was one of my riders. You'll come in or I'll take you myself."

The flare of hatred for Anders that rose in Rae then was almost too great to contain. But the man was smart all right—oh, he was clever as a lobo wolf. Use Will to make the arrest, whip him up until the kid was half-crazy with excitement. And Anders knowing all the time that Rae would hold his hand, not go up against his half brother.

He was whipsawed, and there was nothing he could do. "All right," he heard himself say, still with that surprising coolness. "All right, I'll come in."

Crystal rose from her chair. "I swear to you—" Her voice shook.

"Hush, Crystal," Rae said again, and he raised his hands.

Anders gave a grunt of satisfaction and moved in quickly, fishing the gold-worked Colt from Rae's holster. He looked at it and then at Crystal, his mouth twisting. Then he tossed it to Will. "Hang on to this. I want it for a souvenir."

"Cleve Anders," Crystal said quietly, but with an undertone of dreadful hatred, "as long as there's breath in you, you had better be afraid of me . . ."

"I'm not afraid of any woman," Anders grinned. "Or in your case, maybe the word *slut* suits better."

Rae tensed; a gun muzzle rammed his back. "Stand hitched," the marshal grunted. "That's enough, Cleve."

"Always like to give things their right name," Anders said. He whirled. "Okay, it's enough of palaver. Let's take him over and lock him up. Only it's a damn shame we can't hang the skunk right now. Clyde Brennan was a good man."

"Anders," Rae said in a tone so soft it was hardly audible, "you may not be afraid of Crystal, but you had better be afraid of me. Because now, if I ever git the chance, I'll blow a hole in you on sight."

"Buddy, you're goin' where you won't blow no holes in nothin'." Anders said. He pulled his gun and rammed it hard into Rae's side. With a big hand he gave Rae a shove that nearly rocked him off his feet. "Git movin'."

It was midweek and early in the day and Rae Marsh was the only tenant of the small, tight jail tacked on as a lean-to behind the marshal's office. As the procession, Anders in front, then Rae, then the marshal and Will, both with drawn guns, entered the office, a burly, black-bearded man got to his feet from where he had been dozing in a tilted-back chair in the corner. He was almost apelike in build, freakishly long arms suspending his ham-sized hands at the level of his knees. His hair was a dirty-looking black shag that hung touseled over a low forehead. There was a star on his shirt.

"Ya got 'im, huh?" His voice was a thick rumble.

"We got him, Boze." Anders' voice rang with triumph. "Now it's up to you to see he don't git away. You *sabe*?"

Boze grinned, revealing yellow teeth. "They don't nobody leave thisahere jail until they're turned loose er stretch rope. Don't worry, Mister Anders, Boze ain't never lost a prisoner." One big hand reached out, seized Rae by the slack of the back of his shirt. "'Sides, I always kinda liked Clyde Brennan. Git in thar, you!" He shoved Rae through a cell door with such force that Rae lurched all the way across the tiny space and slammed into the log wall. Boze clanged shut the steel-barred door and turned a big key in the padlock that fastened it. "Don't you worry none at all, Mr. Anders. He'll stay here long as you want 'im."

"See that he does." Anders fished in his pocket; a gold double eagle glittered in the air briefly and Boze caught it. "The day we take him out an' hang him, there's another one just like it," Anders said.

"That'll sure be a fine day," Boze said.

The marshal looked from Boze to Anders. "Cleve," he said, "the town pays Boze."

"Not enough to keep him awake twenty-four hours a day," Anders said. "That's how I want this lousy murderer watched."

The marshal made a hoarse, disgusted sound. "All right."

Anders looked at him, a faint grin on his face. "You don't sound happy, Ira. What's the matter? Ain't you forgot somethin'?"

"I ain't forgot anything," the marshal snapped.

"Oh, yeah you have. You forgot I'm Cleve Anders. That's a bad thing for a man to forgit. Especially when he holds public office in Bent's Crossing."

The marshal had the look of a man trying to gather the remnants of his manhood. "You never helped me in no election. It was John Marsh—"

"But John Marsh is dead," Anders said coldly. "And I'm the he-coon in Fletcher's Hole now. And that's somethin' you don't ever want to forgit, Ira—not ever." His eyes locked with those of the marshal; the lawman met them only for an instant and then turned away.

"We'll take good care of him," he muttered.

"I don't want you to take good care of him," Anders grinned. "I want you to make life miserable fer him. But keep him locked up." He laughed. "Come on, Will. We done a good mornin's work. I'll stand the bunch of you to a drink."

"I got things to do here," the marshal said.

Anders frowned. "I swear, Ira, you're gittin' hard to live with. Didn't you hear me say I'd stand you to a drink?

The marshal raised a hand and dropped it. "Oh . . . hell, all right." He followed as they all filed out, leaving Rae and Boze alone.

Rae looked around him at the cell.

Its walls were of square-hews, close-fitted logs, each a full twelve inches through, with no gaps between them. A tiny window, not more than eight inches by eight inches, had been notched out at a height well above a man's head; it was the only break in that solid wall. The floor was of rock slabs sunk deep in dirt, and the hand-made cell door was a massive affair with a giant padlock through a hasp guaranteeing that only a key would open it. There was a slop bucket and a couple of filthy blankets in one corner on the floor, no other furnishings.

And Anders was worried enough about his escaping from this escape-proof hole to pay a man twenty dollars to keep constant watch on him! For the first time Rae realized just how afraid Anders was of him. . . .

But that was small consolation now. He began to pace the narrow confines of the cell like some captured animal. He forgot Anders in the bitterness of self-disgust and self-hatred with which he lashed himself.

He had been a fool, a first-class fool all along. A fool to try to take on an outfit like Circle M; a fool to trust an outlaw like Tom Ford. Only one good thing had come out of all this mess—Crystal. As he thought how she had lied, sacrificing her reputation, to save him, he stopped pacing, filled for a moment with a warmth of a kind that was strange to him. If she had gone that far for him, maybe she was not quite so indifferent to him after all. Maybe he even dared hope—

Hope? He jeered at himself for thinking the word. Hope? Locked up in an escape-proof hole? With Anders determined that he would hang? And with Anders drawing water enough so that any trial would be only a formality? Hope? He cursed himself under his breath.

"I wish you'd stop that damn pacin'," Boze growled from outside the cell door. He had dragged his chair around to where he could see everything that went on in Rae's cell, and there was a sawed-off double-barreled shotgun cradled in one long arm. "It makes me jumpy."

Rae's bitterness welled over. "You go to hell," he snapped.

Boze got slowly up out of the chair, his little black eyes glittering. "Now, friend," he growled, "you done let yourself in fer trouble, talkin' that way to me. I don't let no prisoner in this here calaboose speak disrespectful to Boze. I reckon you got to be taught a lesson." He cocked the shotgun. Holding it in one hand, his finger on the trigger, he fished a key from his pocket. Grinning through his beard, he unlocked the cell door.

"You wouldn't be smart to jump me," he growled. "It wouldn't take but one little jerk of my finger t' spray this cell with enough lead to cut you plumb in two." Fumbling behind his back, he re-locked the cell. "Now," he said, advancing on Rae, "turn around and stand up there in the corner, like a little boy's been bad in school."

Rae just stood there. He was half on the verge of making a desperate try. But the twin bores of that shotgun advancing on him brought him back to sanity. He wouldn't have a chance.

"Didn't you hear me?" Boze grated. "I said, into that corner. Face first." He made a thrusting motion with the shotgun. Rae saw little flecks of froth and spittle at the corners of his mouth, wetting his beard. There was a glitter in his eyes that was far from sane. He was aching, Rae realized, to use that shotgun, and if he did, far from being reprimanded, Anders would probably reward him.

Slowly, tensely, Rae turned, facing into the corner.

"Fine," Boze grunted. "Now jest stand there. Real still—"

Rae almost screamed with pain then. Boze had reversed the shotgun, slammed the butt of it with terrific force just over Rae's right kidney. His legs sagged, he tried to twist, but then the gunbutt slammed him on the other side and the room spun and whirled crazily. He felt his knees crumpling.

Then he was on all fours on the floor. It was all he could do to keep from sobbing in agony.

"Mebbe that'll teach yuh to listen when I talk," Boze said, his voice rich with satisfaction. Dimly, Rae heard the cell door slam behind him, the key turn in the lock. "It just don't pay to be disrespectful to Boze. . . ."

Rae stayed there on hands and knees for a long time, deathly sick. At last he crawled across the cell and collapsed on the filthy blankets. It seemed forever before the pain began to ebb, his swirling head to clear. As rationality returned, he made one vow, If he ever got a chance at Boze, he would show the jailer no more mercy than Boze had shown him.

IX

THE TWENTY-FOUR hours that crawled by after that were the longest hours that Rae Marsh had ever spent in his life. Half of that time he was sick with the blows the jailer had slammed into his back. He lay on the two foul blankets on the hard floor, rousing himself only long enough to accept the weak coffee and fried potatoes and beef that Boze shoved through the door.

The food helped; he had not eaten since the afternoon before the raid. He could feel his sickness diminish a little, some strength flow back into him, and his mind began to work again and take stock of his situation.

One thing was certain—he had to get out of here. If he came to trial, they would hang him, though all he was morally guilty of was taking cattle that really belonged to him. But, he thought grimly, there was also a good chance he would not come to trial. It was not likely Anders would wait that long. After all, with marshal and jailer both under his thumb, it would be a simple matter for him to raise a lynch mob. There was no time to waste, Rae knew: he had to escape. But how?

It seemed to be impossible. Whoever had built

the jail had built well; it would take a working party and plenty of tools to open a hole big enough to
get through. One man alone had no chance—certainly not with Boze watching him day and night.

For the ape-like jailer was keeping his bargain
with Cleve Anders. He sat perpetually in that chair
in front of the cell, the shotgun across his lap. Occasionally he dozed, but like a cat; let Rae so much
as scuff his boot across the floor and Boze was
awake, the gun coming up even as he opened his
eyes.

Rae slept fitfully through the night that passed,
rousing himself occasionally, hoping that Boze
would be sound asleep, hoping that he'd have a
chance to test the cell for the one chink in its
soundness that was probably not there, but which
was his only forlorn hope. But each time he came
awake, Boze was awake, too.

"You gonna sit like that from now to the trial?"
Rae asked him bitterly once. "Your tail's gonna git
mighty tired of that chair."

Boze's yellow teeth showed in the mat of his
beard.

"I don't figure I'll hafta sit here too damn long,"
he said.

"When's the trial?" Rae asked.

"Trial?" Boze grinned. "Who said anything
about a trial?"

Rae lay back down. Crystal was his only hope—
and what could Crystal do? It was a cinch that she
would not be let anywhere near him. She was probably being watched, probably was as helpless as he.
Besides, he did not want her to take any more
chances on his behalf. She had exposed herself to
enough risk already.

* * *

Daybreak came; he could tell by the shaft of light that lanced through the tiny window overhead.

The marshal arrived with breakfast. He gave it to Boze and Boze shoved it through to Rae. "Eat hearty," he said cryptically. "While you can."

"Where's the marshal?" Rae asked. "I want to talk to him." The lawman had gone out again after bringing the food.

"Ira? Oh, well, it's a funny thing," Boze said. He had dragged up a table and was wolfing his own breakfast as if he hadn't seen food in a month. "Seems like Ira suddenly discovered he had business outa town today. Said he'd be gone all day. Told me to keep a real good watch on you. Which I'm gonna do. Then come nightfall, I reckon I'll buck the tiger a little. Forty simoleons is a nice stake; I jest might run it up."

Rae ate slowly. So today was the day. The marshal out of town to keep his own skirts clear. Boze figuring on having another twenty dollars from Anders tonight, his task completed. The food seemed to clog Rae's throat. By nightfall, unless some miracle occurred, he'd be swinging at the end of a rope.

"You know," Boze went on, "it's a real surprise how many folks in this town thought the world of Clyde Brennan. He never seemed real popular whilst he was alive. But I reckon you never miss th' water till th' well's run dry. An' ole Clyde, I reckon he's about the most popular man in Bent's Crossin' today. You ought to have picked somebody else to bushwhack. Then folks wouldn't be so stirred up, mebbe. Way it is, I wouldn't be surprised if the market fer rope in this town didn't go way up."

Rae said nothing.

"You know, hit's a funny thing about hangin's," Boze went on. "I seen many a man hanged in my time. Now, you take a legal hangin', it ain't so bad on the bird that stretches rope. I mean, where they go to the trouble of buildin' a gallows and all. A legal hangin', the *hombre* drops through th' trap and if th' noose is right, hit breaks his neck when he comes to th' end of th' rope. He don't know what hit him. But a lynchin', that's somethin' dif-ferent. Generally, they don't even bother with a hangman's knot. They just build a plain ole loop, with the rope end through the hondo, and slip it around th' feller's neck. Then they hoist him up over a tree limb an' let him choke to death slow. Or even if they pull a wagon or a horse out from under him, generally there ain't no slack in the rope and he jest hangs there. A man hung that way, he dies slow an' hard. You kin see him turn blue, little by little." Boze gulped another mouthful of meat and talked around it. "I seen it take a man five, ten minutes to die that way. 'Course, if he's lucky, maybe the crowd will use him fer target practice an' put him outa his misery."

Rae looked at Boze with a hatred that was sec-ond only to the hatred he felt for Cleve Anders.

"So they're gonna hang me today," he said qui-etly.

"Wouldn't be surprised," Boze said, chewing.

"Boze," Rae said, "you're a skunk, do you know that? You're about the lowest thing I ever met. I'm surprised you walk on two feet instead of crawlin' on all fours or on your belly. You better hope they hang me today, because if they don't and I ever get a chance, I'll step on you like I would a snake."

Boze chuckled. "That ain't gonna do you no good. You can't make me mad enough to put you outa your misery now. Besides, I wouldn't wanta cheat Mr. Anders that way. But I'll tell you whut— I'll bear a hand on the rope when they swing you, jest so you won't die lonesome." He turned away and went on eating, scraping his plate.

Rae forced himself to down his own food, knowing he was going to need all the strength at his command. Nobody was going to take him out of this jail without a fight, at any rate.

Boze stood up, wiping his mouth with the back of his hand. "There's more 'taters if you want 'em." He picked up his plate and cup, and at that moment the door of the marshal's office opened. Boze dropped the tinware and reached for his shotgun. Then he relaxed. "Oh, it's you," he said. "Howdy, Mr. Marsh."

Will Marsh's voice said, "Mornin', Boze. You still got that backshooter locked up good?"

"Locked up tighter'n a drum."

"Fine," Will said. "Come nightfall, he'll know better than to backshoot a Circle M man."

"Come nightfall, he might not know anything at all," Boze chuckled. "Ain't that right?"

Will's voice had brought Rae to his feet. Now he was at the cell door, gripping the iron bars. There was a faint flutter of hope within him, but it died as Will's voice went on, though the speaker was out of Rae's eyeshot.

"All I'll say," Will said, "is that Cleve and I both have had a belly full of 'im. It was bad enough when he come in here with a cock-and-bull story about havin' some claim on the place. But when he starts rustlin' our beef and then tops it off by shootin' one of our men, I'm past havin' any sympathy for him at all, no matter what kind of wild story he tells. How much was it Cleve promised you if you kept a good eye on him?"

"Mr. Anders give me twenty. Promised me twenty more later."

"Well, I'll add another twenty of my own. Here."

Rae turned away from the bars, with a sickness that had nothing to do with the treatment Boze had given him. Anders had done a thorough job of warping Will's mind, all right. Will was disclaiming him totally, as half borther, as having any right to Circle M, any justification for what he had done. Will was his enemy now, dead set against him—and that was one more thing he owed Anders, one more sum added to the total that now he'd never get a chance to pay.

"Well, now, that's mighty white of yuh, Mr. Marsh. I always said I never seen another outfit good as Circle M. You folks sure take care of your own."

"You damn well betcha," Will said. He moved into view now, sitting on the table on which Boze had breakfasted. He picked up the coffee pot and shook it. "Any more coffee?"

"Sorry. Jest finished it."

"Well, why don't you step across the street an' git another pot? I ain't had my breakfast yet, but I thought I'd better come by and make sure our bird hadn't flown."

Boze looked doubtful. "I got orders—"

Will snorted and picked up the riot gun. He snicked back the hammers and pointed it toward the cell. "I brought him in yesterday," he said. "He won't git past me today."

"Well, shore," Boze said. "If it was anybody but you—I'll be back in three minutes." He took the coffee pot and went out.

As he passed through the door, Will grinned thinly at Rae. "Well, you sleep good last night, bushwhacker?"

"I didn't kill Clyde Brennan," Rae said, getting to his feet. "Dammit, even if nobody else'll believe me, you got to—"

The door closed behind Boze.

Suddenly Will slipped off the table. He eased the shotgun hammers down. "I don't know what to believe," he said quickly, his voice suddenly tremulous. "But I know this—they're gonna lynch you today. Cleve spent last night spreadin' the word, and he's busy again this mornin' gittin' 'em all together."

"And," asked Rae softly, "will it make *you* happy to see me swing?"

Will moved up close to the cell door. "I brought you in yesterday because I figured you might have killed one of my men. But I figured you'd have a trial and a chance to speak your piece. I didn't figure they'd swing you the next day."

Suddenly his hand went inside his shirt. "Here," he said, and he brought out Crystal's gold-plated Colt. "It's got six rounds in it."

Rae took it and rammed it inside his shirt in a smooth motion. Exultation flared in him at the feel of the cold steel. He had a chance now—six cartridges against the town, but a chance. Warmth surged through him. "Will," he said. "I thank you."

Will's eyes met his. "Don't thank me," he said quietly. "Thank John Marsh. You may be his son and you may not; I don't know yet. But I can't take a chance. I can't let you swing without a trial when you may be my father's son, too." He licked his lips. "All I ask is that if you do git clear, you leave this place." His voice shook. "For God's sake, clear out and don't ever come back, you hear?"

"Maybe I will," Rae said quietly. "And maybe I won't. I can't promise you that."

He and Will looked at each other for a moment, and there was misery on the faces of both of them. Then, catlike, Will stepped back to the table and scooped up the shotgun. He snicked back the hammers.

"Well," he grated, "there's one thing certain—you ain't gonna cause any more trouble for Circle M."

And as those words left his mouth, the office door opened and Boze's boots clomped on the floor.

"Everything all right, Mr. Marsh?" He loomed into sight, setting down a pot of steaming coffee and a cup on the table.

"Everything's fine," Will said, lowering the riot-gun's hammers and handing it to Boze. "He's your pigeon again now."

"Not fer long," Boze grinned. "Wheew. This town is jest like a beehive a bear's stirred up. I figure within an hour, neither one of us'll have to worry about keepin' an eye on him."

"The sooner the quicker," Will said, pouring a cup of coffee. He drank it quickly, though it was scalding hot, and set down the cup. "Much obliged, Boze. You ever give up jailing, you come on out and work for us on Circle M. We've got a good place for a man like you."

"Well, now, that's mighty nice," Boze grinned. "But if I kin jest keep on avergin' sixty bucks a prisoner, it'll be too profitable to give up."

Will started for the door. "Don't get spoiled, Boze," he said wryly, and then he went out.

Rae stood there in the corner of the cell, his heart hammering. So the mob was already forming. There was no time to waste. He had no plan— he'd have to play it by ear, improvise. He looked at Boze, who was staring at the coffee pot. "Damn funny—sends me out for coffee and don't drink but one cup."

Rae drew in a deep breath. "Well, since you got a whole pot left, you reckon you could spare me another cup?"

Boze grinned wickedly. "If I didn't know you had less than a hour to live, I wouldn't give you th' sweat off my elbow. But I'd hate fer you to be complainin' about the service in my jail when they took you out. Here, jest to show I'm a good feller, you can have the whole damn' pot. I've drunk enough coffee to where I don't want to see no more."

But he knew his business. He held the shotgun at the ready in one hand and with the other set the coffee pot by the cell door. Still holding the gun pointed at Rae, he unlocked the cell, then stooped and picked up the coffee pot and thrust it through the cracked-open door. "Here you are, friend."

Rae reached for the pot. Then he suddenly slammed both palms upward under its bottom— hard.

The lid of the pot flew open as it jolted upward;

scalding coffee, a brown sheet of it, splashed full into Boze's face.

The man dropped the pot, clawed at his eyes. He howled a curse, stepping backward, and in that fraction of time when he was blinded, Rae threw himself against the cell door and knocked it outward, dragging the golden gun from his shirt.

He brought the gunbarrel down hard across Boze's thick wrists; the shotgun dropped as bone crunched. Boze screamed and reached for his Colt, but he was still blinded, ineffectual. Rae raised the gun again; it came down with crushing force on Boze's thick shag of hair.

Boze's Colt never cleared leather. Rae had put every ounce of strength into that blow, and Boze gave a strange rasping sigh. Blood started from his nostrils, and he collapsed like an empty sack, sprawling full-length on the floor.

Panting, trembling a little with excitement and urgency, Rae stooped and unbuckled Boze's gun belt. He shucked the Colt out of it and stuck it into his waistband. Then he cinched the belt around his own waist and dropped the golden Colt into the holster. Boze was still breathing, still alive, but Rae was satisfied that he had evened the score for the beating with the shotgun butt. It would be a long time before Boze would be in shape to abuse another prisoner.

Grinning tautly and without mirth, Rae strode across the office and cracked the front door. Peering through the crack, he saw with a flare of hope that there was a hitchrack nearby, two saddled horses at it. One of them, a sorrel, was a fine animal, looking as if it had both speed and bottom. There was a Circle M brand on its hip and Rae wondered if Will Marsh had tethered it there.

All right; now he'd have to move fast. But not too fast. He opened the door wide, stepped out onto the sidewalk. In a couple of paces, he was at the hitchrack. The reinknot was loose; he slipped it easily. It took all the self control he had to walk almost casually around to the stirrup and prepare to mount—and his restraint was not made any easier by the fact that he had spotted a knot of men at the head of the street, twenty or thirty of them in a cluster, talking loudly and drifting slowly toward the marshal's office. One of them was waving a coiled rope.

But in a way they had made his escape easier, too. As if not wanting to be involved, everyone else was off the street. Rae swung into the saddle, wheeled the sorrel around. He felt enormous, exposed, vulnerable. He cocked his heels, then brought spurs against the sorrel's flanks hard.

That was when they spotted him. As the sorrel broke into a lurching run, a shout went up from the crowd. Somebody bawled: "Hey, look yonder! Ain't that—?" And somebody else yelled: "Hell, it's Marsh! He's got away!"

As the sorrel pounded down the street, Rae risked a look back over his shoulder. The men behind him were scattering for horses, but some of them were dragging guns, too. Rae crouched low and lashed the sorrel with the reins. As he did so, gunfire splattered in a ragged burst behind him and he heard the vicious rip of bullets close by his head.

Then he was at the end of the street, and he turned the sorrel obliquely to put the shelter of buildings between himself and the lynch mob. But as the sorrel pounded across the open flat, Rae looked back again and saw mounted men pouring after him. His start was scanty—and now everything depended on the horse beneath him, its speed and its endurance.

He was almost certain now that Will had put the horse there—luck alone could never have provided him with such a mount.

Slowly but surely, its pounding hoofs widened the gap between Rae and his pursuers. They were firing at him from horseback, but that was wasted lead; only a lucky shot could hit him. And so far nobody had thought to rein in and use a rifle.

But as the sorrel pulled him out of sixgun range, somebody did have that thought. A bullet whined by Rae's head, too close, and he looked back. Two of the pursuers were dismounted, kneeling, tracking him with carbines. He jerked the sorrel around, zig-zagging it, in a maneuver that cost him ground. But though another couple of bullets ripped close, none found its mark.

He had to get into the hills, into the badlands; there was no other place in which he had a chance of losing them. There was no carbine on his saddle, and he could not hope to make a stand with a sixgun—flight was his only chance.

The ground flowed beneath the sorrel's ironshod hoofs and still the pursuers kept on, though they were dropping farther and farther behind. Ahead loomed the blue range of hills. Then the sorrel was climbing, laboring up a slope for the cover of a grove of pines; they gained it, and in its shelter, Rae pulled it in, gave it a moment to breathe. He drew the gold-plated gun and snapped a trio of shots towards the posse. They were barely within the maximum range of the cartridge and he had no hope of hitting anything, but maybe a little fighting back would slow them down; there was something about the sound of lead that had a sobering effect.

He was startled but jubilant when a horse reared and began to plunge, stung by a bullet, throwing its rider. The pursuers drew rein for a moment, blocked by the crazed animal. Rae jigged the sorrel hard and it plunged on up the slope.

It was panting when it crested the ridge, but Rae showed it no mercy. He put it at a skittering slide down the needle slick hill, heading for the mouth of a rocky draw below. He knew that draw, as he knew all of Fletcher's Hole now; it would lead him into rough country where he could be lost from sight. When, instead of chasing him by eye, like greyhounds after a coyote, they had to track him through bad terrain where each twist and turn might lead them into ambush, he did not think they would be so determined in their pursuit.

They were coming over the ridge behind him now; he could hear their shouting. But he was in brush; it closed behind him in a thick screen, whipping his face, clawing at his chaps. He covered his eyes with an arm, and would not let the sorrel slow, though thorn and stub ripped its silky hide.

Then he knew he was lost to their sight; he turned off into a smaller draw, where the tiring sorrel stumbled over treacherous rock. Only when he had twisted and turned through a labyrinthine maze of draws and gullies and had emerged into a narrow canyon that would lead him toward the real badlands in the direction of the river did he allow the sorrel another breather.

While it panted with distended nostrils, he

looped its reins around a limb and climbed up the
canyon a way on foot. There he listened; he could
hear no sounds of pursuit. But the silence did not
lull him into any false security; he knew Cleve Anders too well to think that he would give up this
easily. He would throw every man he could recruit
into the search; they would beat the country for
him like hunters after a mad wolf.

And, he told himself, right now there was nowhere else to go but to Tom Ford.

X

EVEN AFTER the lookout had passed him on into Ford's sanctuary, Rae rode slowly, thoughtfully, watchfully. He could not count on a red-carpet reception from Ford. Not after the way the man had double-crossed him in the matter of the execution of Clyde Brennan. Ford would be expecting trouble out of Rae on account of that, and until the matter was settled between them, Rae knew it would be well to be on his guard.

But he made it on through to Ford's main ranch without any difficulty. There were cattle grazing on the flat he had to cross to reach it—cattle that had once been Circle M stock but now bore a Circle Double Diamond brand, with the lower halves of the diamond still raw and unhealed.

They had seen him coming, and when he pulled up in front of the long log building, Ford was standing in the doorway, a couple of men behind him.

"Howdy, Marsh," the lean rustler said. "What brings you in here?"

"We'll talk about it in a minute," Rae said. "What about havin' somebody grain my horse?"

"Mac," Ford said, jerking his head, and one of

his men took the sorrel's reins and led it to the corral. Ford's eyes swept over the animal and then back to Rae. "You been ridin' hard," he said.

"Had to," Rae answered. "I just broke jail in Bent's Crossing yesterday."

Ford tensed. "You jest what?"

"You heard me," Rae said.

Ford stood aside to let him in the house, followed him. Ford and his men weren't taking their eyes from him.

"Seems," Rae said slowly, "that after you turned that Circle M man loose the other night, somebody bushwhacked him. Shot him in the back and left his body out on the range to be found. They come and took me in for it. Yesterday they got up a necktie party, but I managed to bust out before they could swing me."

"You mean somebody shot that feller we turned loose?" Ford tried to put surprise in his voice, but it rang false.

"I said that, didn't I?" Rae snapped. "And even left him where he could be found. Almost like they wanted to see the murder pinned on me." He reached behind him for another biscuit. "Because I didn't know he was dead and there I was, a sittin' duck, when Anders and the marshal walked in."

"I see," Ford said. He walked over to a table and sat down and uncorked a bottle. "Well, come on over and have a drink and we'll talk about it."

"Yeah," Rae said, "I think we ought to." He sat down across from Ford, but he did not put his feet under the table; he sat slewed around so his back could be to the wall.

He took the drink Ford pushed toward him and gulped it down. He was dog-tired, and it helped him slough off some of his fatigue. But when Ford offered him another, he shook his head.

"All right," Ford said after a minute. "I had Joe follow that Circle M rider and shut his mouth." He looked directly at Rae with cold eyes. "If you'd let me handle it the way I wanted to to begin with, there wouldn't have been any trouble. Nobody would ever have found his body. But Joe didn't catch up with him until he was back on Circle M land and there wasn't time to hide him right."

"I didn't want him killed at all," Rae said harshly.

Ford sucked in a long breath, a sort of sigh. "Marsh," he said, "there's one thing we ought to git straight. You thought up this deal and set it up, and you done a good job on that. But when it comes to liftin' cattle, you're an amateur. I'm a professional. I know my business, and part of my business is to see that nobody lives to spread even a scrap of information about the way I operate. Now, I didn't want to have to fight with you the other night. I like you, like you fine. But I couldn't let that waddy go loose to shoot off his mouth. You git chicken-hearted in this business, the next thing you know, you find yourself decorating a limb."

Rae said nothing.

"Now you're on th' dodge," Ford said. "But if you'd let me handle it right from the first, you wouldn't be." He poured himself another drink. "Next time, you'll trust my judgment."

"There's not gonna be any next time," Rae said.

Ford sat up straight. "What do you mean?"

"I mean," Rae said, "we've got all we're gonna take."

Ford's brows drew together. "My pipeline ain't nowhere near full yet. I can handle another two hundred, three hundred head easy."

"You couldn't get 'em without fighting for 'em," Rae said. "Fletcher's Hole is stirred up like a hornet's nest. You'd have to pay in blood for every steer you got. Or somebody would."

Ford was silent for a moment. "So you're callin' off your war with Cleve Anders," he said finally. "He's got you buffaloed, huh?"

"Listen," Rae said sharply. "I went into this thing because by rights one third of all Circle M cattle belongs to me. What I was doin' was hirin' you to take what was mine anyhow. I don't call that rustlin', and I don't call that wrong. But when it comes to cold-blooded murder, to shootin' a man in the back or cuttin' his throat like a hog—"

"Then you go soft," Ford finished for him.

"Then I draw the line," Rae said evenly. "So we're goin' to stop now. Before anybody else gits killed."

"My boys ain't scared," Ford said.

"We've been lucky so far," Rae went on. "Three hundred cattle, and even at hot prices, that's three thousand dollars, and nobody's got hurt except Brennan, and that wasn't my doin'. I wanted to git some money to carry this fight into court and git clear title; once I had that, nobody could do anything about me taking my own stock. But you've ruined that for me now, Ford. You brought murder into it, and now I'm on the dodge and I can't even show my face, much less get into court. So what good is liftin' any more cattle gonna do me now? The rest of the operation's off, and that's that."

Ford looked at him for a long moment. Then the rustler shrugged. "If that's the way you feel about it. What do you aim to do now?"

Rae relaxed a little; he had not expected Ford to agree so readily. But probably Ford, who balanced everything off in profit and loss, agreed with Rae's estimate of the situation—that he could not take any more cattle without having to fight for every head.

"What am I gonna do?" Rae repeated. "I'm not sure yet."

"You can throw in with us if you want to," Ford said. "There's another basin south of here I've been aimin' to work. This might be the right time."

"No," Rae said. "No, thanks." His lip curled bitterly. "Like you said. I'm an amateur. I reckon I'll stay one."

"Then what? You gonna hightail it out, let Anders have your piece of the spread?"

Rae stood up. "No," he said, "I'm not gonna do that, either." His voice was harsh, bitter. "I'm not through fightin' Anders. I owe him too much to call off my own personal war now. I may never get my piece of Circle M, but before I pull out of this range, I'm going to pay Anders back as much as I can for what he's put me through."

"By yourself?" Ford's brows arched.

"By myself," Rae said, and there was determination in his tone.

There were things he had needed, and he got them from Ford. Grub. Spare cartridges for his six-gun. A carbine and scabbard and shells. Blankets. The rustler seemed to go out of his way to be helpful. "Like I said," he told Rae, "I'm a businessman. When your share of the money's on hand, I'll leave word for you in the usual place." That was a hollow tree Rae and Ford had used as a post office, in the hills behind Circle M range. "And if you need any other supplies in the meantime, let me know."

"I appreciate it," Rae said. But he was glad to be clear of Ford and his outfit. Contact with them had left him feeling smeared and dirty. Or, he thought, maybe it was the entire situation that made him feel that way. Every aspect of it was rotten. Sometimes when he thought of what might have been, of the way things could have been if John Marsh had just lived a few days longer or if he had just reached Circle M a few days earlier, the grief and bitterness of it racked him. It could all have been so simple, so easy, with no need for this fighting, moonlight raiding, and killing, if only—

If only time had not betrayed him. If only he had come home while John Marsh had still lived.

But he had not, and gradually his plans were taking shape. He had half of the money coming from the three hundred head he had helped Ford rustle. It would be awhile before it came in, because it would take awhile for the blotted brands to heal. He had no compunction about taking that money —rightfully it belonged to him anyway; it was only a fraction of what should truly been his. And it would not be enough to buy any spread in New Mexico. But he would wait here for it—two weeks, a month, however long it took. He would wait here, and in the meantime, he would do his best to make Cleve Anders' life hell on earth.

And afterwards . . . after he had the money . . .

Well, then he would drift. Maybe he would use

the money to go to South America, get a clean start there. Or someplace where he was not known. But, he thought bitterly, he would have to go alone. He had dreamed of taking Crystal with him when he left Fletcher's Hole. But that dream was shattered now. Even if she would come, he had no right to ask her, no right even to tell her that he loved her —and he knew now that he did. Because he was an outlaw, and Anders would see that he remained an outlaw.

All these things he thought about as he holed up in a small dirt cave in the cleft of a dry streambed back in the hills. He had plenty of time to think; as he had expected, Anders had all the able-bodied men he could lay hands on out beating the countryside for him. Well, he would give them time to give up, become discouraged, decide he had left the Hole. Then, when things had died down, he would strike.

A week passed, and a careful reconnaissance showed him that the manhunt had died away.

It was time to begin war against Anders again.

His first move was comparatively innocuous. He watched a Circle M line-camp until its two occupants, who had been put out there to keep watch against rustlers, were out on patrol. Then he rode down, took what he needed from it, and poured the contents of the coal-oil can on the floor. A flicked match set the log shack to burning like tinder.

That was on the north side of Circle M. He spent all the next day riding a half-circle through the hills. Nightfall found him on the south side. This part was used for a hay ranch. Circle M's winter fodder had been cut and dried and piled. That night it all went up in flame and smoke, along with all the deserted hay ranch buildings.

Cowman that he was, Rae both hated to do that and took grim satisfaction in it. It hurt to see the good hay burning, but it did not hurt to think about the bind it would put Anders in, having to buy an entire winter's feed. Rae knew the burning of the hay would be a body blow to Anders; Circle M would feel it.

Circle M felt it, all right. Again its range swarmed with armed riders.

But they were no match for one man working alone, one man who moved under cover of darkness, prepared to take desperate chances. A man who could cut miles of wire in a night, a man who could burn one line camp after another, a man who could ease into the home ranch itself, infiltrating Anders' carefully placed guards, set fire to the hay and grain stored there and even to the cookshack, fire a volley of harassing shots without intent to kill, and still escape while Circle M men swarmed toward the flames like excited moths.

Because what Rae Marsh had set out to do was burn Circle M bit by bit. He could not burn the cattle, and he could not burn the land itself, but all the rest was vulnerable. Buildings would burn. Dry range would burn. And scarcely a night passed now that the darkness did not suddenly blossom into orange somewhere on Circle M. . . .

He could measure the effectiveness of the job he was doing, the havoc he wreaked, by the number of riders combing the hills. Anders had kept on the gunslingers he had hired at the height of the rustling, and now he drove them in ceaseless man-hunting. In itself, their hire and keep was another drain on Circle M's resources, and Rae smiled grimly to himself at the thought of the size of Anders' payroll.

There were a few close shaves. Once he carelessly skylined himself against the flare of a burning line camp; a rifle barked unexpectedly from the darkness and the bullet sliced the wing of his left chaps leg. Another time, the sorrel's nicker woke him from sleep in a brushy covert just in time to spot two riders hard on him. There was a hot chase before he lost them, and the sorrel took a bullet-burn across a ham; a fraction of an inch deeper and he would have been on foot; they would have had him cold.

But he escaped them. And sooner or later, he always made it back to his cave in the dry streambed, a sanctuary that none of them had come close to, yet.

It was a dismal, exhausting life he led, the life of a hunted killer animal, but he was sustained through it by hatred, and by the determination to burn his share of Circle M rather than let Cleve Anders gloat over it.

Meanwhile, he was glad to see that Tom Ford had kept his promise; he and his rustlers had stayed away from Circle M. Rae had worried about that.

He slept restlessly as a wolf one afternoon in the dirt cave in the bank of the streambed, his carbine cradled in his arm. Last night had been a frustrating one. Anders' men had been out in full force, and Rae had already hit all the easy targets. He had been unable to penetrate that screen of gunmen without having to fight his way through; and so, at last, he had given up and retreated to his cave.

Now something—he didn't know what—brought him wake, upright and instantly alert, lifting the carbine before he knew whether there was anything to aim it at.

For a moment there was no sound, nothing he could hear except the thudding of his own heart, the pulse of blood in his own ears. He was about to lay the carbine aside when it came again, from down the streambed: the click of ironshod hoofs on rock.

Rae bit his lip and jacked a round into the carbine. If this was Anders' men and they found him, he was trapped good, boxed in like a steer in a branding chute. There would be nothing to do but fight his way out or be slaughtered.

He bellied to the edge of the cave, cautiously peered out. All he could see was the crown of a hat bobbing in and out of the brush that choked the vanished creek's empty seam. One hat—but there might be more riders coming.

The sorrel was picketed not far away, but there was no saddle on it. He usually tried to keep it saddled, but constant pressure from a sweaty blanket produced galls, and its back had to air for awhile each day. By the time he could slither down, get to the horse, yank the picket-pin and mount bareback, the strange rider would be upon him. No, he would have to wait, and, if necessary, fight.

The hat came closer. Rae estimated where it would emerge from the wall of brush into a stretch where a rock bottom had kept the streambed clear. He raised the carbine and trained it on that spot, and his finger lapped around the trigger.

The hat moved exactly toward the spot he had a bead on, and now he could see the color of a brush

jacket, get an occasional glimpse of the hide of the
claybank horse the intruder rode. Two seconds
more, one, and the man would be in the clear. . . .

Then the rider came out of the brush.

Rae let out a rasping sigh and dropped the gun
barrel. Suddenly he was trembling. Only the final
crook of a trigger finger had stood between him
and driving a .30-30 slug through his own half
brother.

"Damn," he muttered. "Damn, Will, why did it
have to be you?"

Will came on up the defile, eyes sweeping its
banks. He had a carbine cradled across his saddle
horn. He still wore his crossed gunbelts, the two
Colts tied low. He was only a boy, true enough, but
with all that artillery he looked dangerous.

But maybe, Rae thought hopefully, Will would
miss his sign. The mouth of the cave was lightly
screened by brush, and it was up high with a jutout
of rock and earth beneath it; maybe Will would
ride on by, unseeing.

But that was not to be. From nearby, the picketed sorrel whinnied a shrill welcome to Will's
mount.

Instantly Rae's half brother reined in, raising the
carbine. His eyes moved carefully over the terrain.
They came to rest on the mouth of the cave; and
Rae saw Will stiffen.

Then, in a quick motion, Will was off his horse,
using it for a shield. All Rae could see of him was
hat and the muzzle of the carbine across the saddle.

Will's voice rang through the silence. "All right,
Rae! Come down outa there! Or I'll come up after
you!"

Rae picked up the carbine. Will fired; the roar of the rifle was thunderous; Rae heard the bullet spang off rock far below the cave and knew it was not a shot intended to kill.

Biting his lip, Rae lay frozen for a moment. Then he got to his knees.

"All right! Hold your fire! I'm comin' down!"

If Will had wanted to kill him then, he could have done it. For the moment that he was squeezing through the narrow mouth of the cave, Rae was off-balance and helpless, a perfect target. But the rifle Will held across the saddle did not bark again. In a shower of dirt, rocks, and clods, Rae skittered down the hill. He brought up panting in the bed of the stream.

Will ducked under the horse's neck and straightened up, and then the two half-brothers were facing each other, each with a saddle gun in one hand, each with his other hanging loose near a sixgun.

"You damn' fool," Rae said tensely, after a second's silence. "What made you so blame sure I wouldn't gun you down? I had a bead on you from the minute you come through that brush."

"I wasn't sure," Will said. He was as tense as Rae, his face white, his lips taut. He had sweated all the way through his brush jacket. "How'd you know I wouldn't plug you when you came out through that cave?"

"Wouldn't have been much sense in that," Rae said. "After all, you're the one helped me break jail."

"Maybe that's why I figured you wouldn't plug me," Will said.

They were silent for a moment more, each looking at the other. To look into Will's eyes, Rae thought, was like looking into a mirror. It was uncanny.

Then Rae said, "You're alone." It was a statement, not a question.

"That's right," Will said. "I'm alone. The others hunt in pairs—at least in pairs. But if I found you, I didn't want anybody else along to hear what I got to say."

Rae nodded. "What have you got to say?"

Will looked at him steadily.

"Get off this range," he said. "Or the next time I have a chance, I'm not gonna throw off my shot."

Something cold touched Rae's spine; but there was no doubt from the look in Will's eyes that he meant it.

"I gave you that gun in jail," Will said, " 'cause I didn't want to see you murdered without a fair trial. But I asked you then, dammit, to clear out. And you didn't do it."

"No," Rae said. "I didn't."

"Instead, you're burnin' Circle M up. This is almost worse than the rustling." Will's voice was sharp. "You've forgot one thing. Regardless of what your claim is on the spread, and regardless of how right it might be—and I ain't sayin' it is or ain't—Circle M belongs to me, too. I was born on it and I grew up on it. And I ain't going to stand by and see it destroyed by nobody, half brother or not."

Rae said nothing. But he could see now that he had done more damage than he had intended. Not to Circle M, but to himself. Before, his half brother had been undecided. But Rae's depredations had driven him firmly onto Cleve Anders' side of the fence.

So he had cost himself his most important ally.

"Look," he said desperately, "I'm not making war on you."

"When you make war on Circle M," Will said, "you're making war on me. And that means I got to make war on you." He paused, then went on. "Anyhow, you ain't got a chance. I mean that. Cleve's not gonna give up until he runs you down. And he's put enough of a reward on your head so that you don't dare to show your face to anybody in Fletcher's Hole."

"If Cleve would listen to sense," Rae said, "you coulda bought my share, you and Cleve, for less than this war's cost you so far."

"Cleve ain't listenin' to anything," Will said. "When he gits a hate on, it stays on. I know Cleve from away back. And he hates you worse'n I've ever seen him hate anybody. You've hurt us, Rae, hurt us bad. Range burned up, winter feed burned up . . . we can't hold over the winter. We're havin' to make a special gather right now and sell off five hundred head when the market's down, but if we don't do that, they'll starve or break us buyin' feed. Cleve ain't happy about that. Neither am I. Now, I'm gonna ask you one more time. Ride out. Let this rustlin' and burnin' stop. Then maybe I can do somethin' in your behalf. But if it don't stop . . . well, then, I'm comin' after you right along with the rest of Circle M."

Rae stared at him for a moment. Then he let out a long breath. He laid down the carbine and sat down on a rock, and took out his makings and rolled a cigarette.

"The rustlin's stopped," he said. "There won't be any more of that. I can promise you. But don't forget, it was my own cattle I stole."

"Maybe so, maybe not," Will said coldly.

"I took 'em," Rae went on, "so I could get enough money to fight this in court. But then Cleve came after me and tried to lynch me and—"

"Don't forget, Clyde Brennan's dead. I never had no love for Clyde; he was always too much Cleve's pet dog, to come when Cleve whistled, and I wouldn't have trusted him no farther than I can spit. But he was a Circle M man and you got him killed."

"I did everything I could to save him," Rae said. "They promised me they were turning him loose. Hell, I was ready to fight 'em if they didn't. But after I thought he'd gone free, they sent a man and bushwhacked him. That was when I told 'em the deal was off. I didn't want anybody else gittin' killed." He lit the cigarette. "You haven't lost any beef since then, have you? Far as I know, they've left you alone."

"We haven't lost any more beef," Will said. "But we've sure as hell lost a lot else—all burned up. And that's got to stop too."

"And if it don't, you'll be comin' after me?"

"That's right," Will said, and something gleamed in his eyes, and suddenly Rae realized that even though the boy hated the idea, he was fascinated by it, too; fascinated by the thought of using those guns he had lugged around for so long and dreamed so many wild dreams about. . . .

Yes, Will would come after him, all right.

Rae took another drag on the cigarette and dropped it into the dirt. He ground it out with the toe of his boot.

"Okay," he said. "The war's over."

Will tensed. "You mean that?"

"Far as I'm concerned," Rae said, gettin to his feet. "I've already called off the rustlers; I'm callin' myself off, too. That don't mean I don't hate Anders' guts, and that don't mean that someday I'm gonna figure out how to get my share of what's comin' to me. My father wanted me to have it, and maybe that means more to me than you can understand. But you brought me that gun in jail because we had the same blood. All right; that's why I'm callin' off my war. Because if you came after me, I'd have to kill you, and I don't want that."

"I don't think you could take me," Will said quickly, defiantly.

"We'll never know," Rae said, filled with a great weariness, a tiredness that seemed to strike to his very bones. "Because I ain't about to try to find out." He raised his head and his voice crackled. "Okay, you can turn and ride now. Go make your beef gather or whatever you got to do."

"What about you?"

"It's a big country," Rae said. "A big world. I'll find someplace."

Will looked at him for a moment. "I wish, dammit—" he began and then left the sentence unfinished. Suddenly he ducked back under the horse's neck and in one smooth motion he was in the saddle. He held the horse close-reined for a moment, looking down at Rae. "Good luck," he said.

"Same to you," Rae said.

Will wheeled his mount, spurred it, and rode

back into the brush. Rae watched him go. Then he turned, wearily, and climbed back up to the cave to pack his gear.

Yes, he thought, the war was over. And he had lost it. He had been defeated by the one thing he could not fight—his father's blood in Will Marsh. He had, for all his efforts, won nothing at all—not the chance to see his father alive, not his father's inheritance to him. And, he thought bitterly, not Crystal, which was the sorest loss of all. But even if she really did feel anything for him, which she had vehemently denied all along, she would not, now. Not after he told her that he planned to turn tail and run, like a whipped dog. Before she had the vengeance for her husband's death that she had linked up with him to seek.

No, he was leaving Crystal in the lurch, too, with no change in Fletcher's Hole except that Cleve Anders would have a free hand now to make things as rough for Crystal as he could—and there was nothing anybody could do about it.

But he would keep his word to Will; he would be riding soon. There was only one thing left to do. He could not just pull out without seeing Crystal again. Somehow, under cover of night, he would have to get into Bent's Crossing.

XI

AT TWO o'clock in.the morning, the town was asleep. On Saturday nights and payday Circle M money would boom the town all night long, but this was midweek, and everything, even the saloons, shut early. As Rae catfooted down the alley behind Crystal's place, no more than a gliding, blacker shadow in pitch darkness, only a stray dog nosing in a pile of garbage noted his passing.

From the alley, a service stair led up to Crystal's rooms over the saloon itself. But, Rae knew, the door at its head would be bolted. And it would take a lot of pounding, attract a lot of attention, to get in that way. He had something else in mind.

Silently, he climbed the stair. At the landing at its top, he paused for a moment. Then he clambered up on the rail that encircled the landing, leaned out and grabbed the roof that covered the landing. It took every ounce of muscle in arms and shoulders to swing himself up.

But from the landing roof, it was only an easy step to the main roof of the false fronted building, and that was as flat as a ballroom floor.

Rae made it and kept low behind the shallow wooden parapet. When he had reached the position he wanted, he leaned over the parapet's edge. Yes, the window was just below him. He slipped the Colt from his holster and unbuckled his cartridge belt. Holding it by the tongue, he lowered it over the parapet. Its massive buckle just reached the upper pane of glass in the window.

He let it swing gently of its own momentum. The metal buckle tapped rhythmically against the glass. Rae held his breath and waited.

Nothing happened. He swung the belt harder. It made a racket now that seemed to him thunderous, that must wake half the town. In a moment, he pulled the belt up.

Then he let out a long breath as he heard the sound of a window sash sliding up. A woman's voice, Crystal's voice, said, puzzled, "What—?"

"Crystal," Rae hissed.

He could see the gleam of white, bare shoulders as she leaned out the window. "What—? Who?"

"Crystal! It's me."

"Rae!" It was an explosive whisper. "Where are you?"

"Up on the roof. Unbolt the back door and let me in."

He heard Crystal catch her breath. Then she whispered: "Right away."

He hurried back across the roof and swung down to the landing. As his boots thudded on the landing floor, Crystal, in a robe, her black hair flowing down her shoulders, pulled open the door. Without pausing, Rae ducked inside. But he was unprepared for what happened next.

Suddenly Crystal's arms were about him, the perfume of her hair strong in his nostrils, as she pressed her head against his chest. "Oh, Rae, oh, darling, I thought . . . I was afraid . . ."

For one fraction of a second, Rae was uncom-
prehending, disbelieving. Then something within
him soared. His arms went around Crystal in an
iron grip; when she raised her face, he kissed her,
and the kiss lasted a long time. . . .

Then Crystal broke loose and pushed the door
shut and bolted it. "I've worried about you so
much. I've been almost out of my mind. No word
from you—and all those men hunting you, and a
reward on your head. . . ."

Rae took her hand. It was warm and soft within
his. His brain was still trying to make sense of all
this, but one thing he already knew—he had not
been defeated after all. Defeat had just turned into
victory.

"Let's go where we can talk," he whispered.

She led him down the hall and they entered the
living room of her apartment. She lit a lamp; then,
as light flooded the room again, she was in his arms
once more. "Oh, I've been going crazy," she
murmured.

For a long time, Rae just held her. Then he released her. "You got any whiskey? I'd like a
drink."

"Yes. Sure. Are you hungry? What do you
want?"

"Just the whiskey," Rae said. His mouth curled.
"And what I've already had. So you missed me,
eh?"

Crystal's cheeks were flaming as she poured the
drink. "I didn't know," she murmured. "Until they
came in while we were sitting there and took you
like that . . . and I thought Cleve Anders was going
to hang you. And there was nothing I could do

about it; they wouldn't let me or anybody else anywhere near the jail. I died a thousand times . . .!"

Rae took the whiskey and sipped it. "And then these past few weeks," she went on. "You out there somewhere all alone, and all those gunmen of Cleve's looking for you. And not a word from you, not a word. Never knowing from one moment to the next whether you were alive or dead . . ." She broke off. "Yes," she said. "I missed you." And her eyes met his.

The warmth that filled Rae was not from the whiskey. But then it ebbed.

"Well, you won't have those worries any longer," he said.

Crystal's brows arched. "What do you mean?"

"I mean I'm beat," Rae said. "I'm giving up. I can fight Anders. But I can't fight Will. And if I keep on, I'll have to." He drained the glass. "I'm sorry, Crystal, I know you've taken a lot of long chances for me—and I've hurt Anders. But not like you wanted me to. Not so bad he can't get well from it."

"Anders," she said huskily. "Do you think I care about Anders anymore? Oh, Rae, I've prayed for you to quit. If I'd had any way to get in touch with you—" She broke off. "I'm just sorry you didn't get what you wanted."

Rae said, softly, "Maybe I got what I wanted after all." Then his voice became crisp. "Crystal, I'm going to have to go away. I've got some money coming from Ford—not much, but a little stake, anyhow. If I take it and find some place where it's quiet and safe and we . . . well, if I sent for you, would you come?"

"Anywhere," she said. "Anywhere. Just so long

as we're away from Anders. If you knew all the nights I've lain awake worrying about him killing you the way he killed Ward Crystal, the way he killed your—" She broke off suddenly, her face gone white. "Let me pour you another drink."

But Rae was on his feet. "Wait a minute," he rasped. "What was that you said?"

Crystal turned a stricken face toward him. "Nothing." Her voice was choked.

"*The way he killed Ward Crystal, the way he killed my*—" Rae stepped around the table. "Crystal, you know something I don't know."

She shook her head frantically. "I don't know anything. All I want is for us to get away from here, for you to be safe."

His hand shot out and seized her arm; he pulled her close to him, fingers digging into soft flesh with an iron grip. He saw her wince with pain.

"Tell me," he rasped. "Tell me what you were about to say!"

Crystal looked up into his cold eyes a moment. Then she let out a long, shuddering, sighing breath. She wrenched her arm away from his grip. "Rae, it would only mean—" Her words trailed off as she saw the expression on his face. Then her shoulders slumped. "All right," she whispered. "All right. But it was only drunk talk."

"I'm listening," Rae said stonily.

Crystal's tongue ran over her lips. "Last night . . . last night Doc Miller was in my place. He's . . . the doctor who tended to your father."

"Go on," Rae said.

"Rae, he's a soak, a drunk; you can't put reliance in what he says."

"Let me be the judge of that."

She was silent a moment, obviously reluctant to continue, but Rae's cold gaze forced her to speak again. "He was talking about ... about your father's last days. He had told everybody the reason John Marsh didn't live sixty, maybe even ninety days longer, was that his heart failed him. But his heart didn't fail him, the doctor said. What happened was ... he took ... or somebody gave him ... an overdose of the dope, the narcotic, that was being used to kill his pain."

An odd iciness moved through Rae Marsh's body. He stood perfectly rigid.

"It was that drug that killed him?"

"That's what Doc Miller said," Crystal whispered almost inaudibly.

"Then why," Rae rapped, "didn't he say so in the first place?"

"He told me that, too," Crystal went on. "He had no way of knowing that you even existed. And John Marsh was in pain and his case was hopeless. The doctor thought maybe he had taken it himself, not wanting to linger on and on and suffer like that."

"He wouldn't have done that," Rae said quickly. "He was waiting for me."

"Doc Miller didn't know that. He thought John just hadn't been able to stand it any longer. Or, if somebody gave it to him, maybe Cleve, maybe Will, it was an act of ... of mercy. He didn't see any need to talk it around."

Rae sat down suddenly, his face working, a chaos of emotion boiling within him. "There's no mercy in Cleve Anders," he grated. "And Will wouldn't have done it." It was all he could do to speak through the grief and rage that gripped him.

"No, my father was murdered. And I know who did it." He balled his hands into fists. "Will said that the day before he died, he whispered something to Cleve. It must have been about me. And Cleve knew that if the old man was still alive when I came home, he'd see that I got my share of Circle M. So it was Cleve that done it, don't you see? It was Cleve that poured that stuff into him . . ." His voice faltered. "And just before I got here, so that he died and was in his grave before I could see him. . . ."

Crystal came to him and knelt, her hand over his. "Darling, I'm sorry. But there's nothing you can do to bring him back. Please, let's—"

Rae flung her hand away savagely and stood up.

Crystal got to her feet and backed away a step. Her face was bone-white.

"No," Rae said. "Not yet."

"What are you going to do?" Crystal whispered.

Rae stood there for a moment without speaking, his hands still knotted into fists. When he finally did break the silence, his voice was quiet, steady, and normal again.

"Why," he said, "I'm going to find Cleve Anders and kill him, that's what I'm gonna do."

Crystal came to him again, put her arms around him. "Rae, please—for my sake. All those gunmen of his . . . you'll never get through them. They'll kill you and—I've already lost one man to Anders . . ."

"I'll get through to him," he said. "Don't worry, somehow I'll get through to him. They haven't made enough lead yet to stop me from getting to him and killing him." His mouth twisted. "It's what I should have done in the first place. It's what

I should have done when I had him down out there in the street and you stopped me. God, if I'd suspected—"

He turned away from her. "Crystal, I'm sorry, but this is something I've got to do. Forget about me. Chalk me off. If I come back, all right. But if I don't, at least you'll be free of Anders." He pulled the gold-plated gun from its holster and turned. "Here. I've got my own in my saddle bag. This belonged to Ward Crystal. You don't want to lose it if something happens to me."

"No." She shook her head violently. "No, keep it, please keep it."

Rae stared at her a moment, then nodded and slid it back into leather. "All right," he said. He started toward the door. "If I'm able to," he said, "I'll come back as soon as I can after it's over. But if I don't, pretend you never knew me." He put his hand on the knob.

"Rae." Her voice halted him.

He turned. "Yes?"

Crystal's face was composed, courageous now. She came to him. "You can kiss me first before you go, can't you?"

Rae looked down at her. Then he smiled faintly.

"Yes," he said. "I can do that."

XII

B<small>UT IT WAS</small> not all that easy.

Though Rae's grim resolve did not lessen one whit, as the night passed, his instinct for self-preservation began to function again and his mind worked more rationally. He would kill Anders, all right; he would do that if he had to walk through a hailstorm of lead to get it done. And he would do it face to face, so that Anders would know who was killing him and why. But there was a force of life warring with that killing urge within Rae, too. Crystal. He had just found her. If at all possible, he wanted to come back to her.

But the thought of her did not weaken him. It only made him more rational.

Long before dawn, he was well concealed in a covert on a slope above the Circle M spread. He watched the ranch house almost unwinkingly. Sooner or later, Anders would have to come out. And wherever he went when he did, wherever he rode to, Rae Marsh would follow him; and there would come a time when Anders would be alone, or at least the odds would be cut down, and that was when Rae would get him. He was prepared to wait, now; his rage had been transformed into cold fury and an icy patience.

Dawn streaked the sky. Circle M came awake, punchers filing out of the bunkhouse to the jerry-built structure that replaced the cook shack Rae had burned. Will emerged from the ranch house to join them; he still wore his two gunbelts and Colts; Rae wondered bitterly if he slept with them.

But Anders did not appear. Breakfast over, there was a catching up of the horses the jingler had brought into the corral, the usual confusion of the first early-morning mounting, with broncs snapping out their kinks under their riders. Rae thought that there were not as many hands at the home ranch as usual; then he remembered why. Most of them were probably out on the range with a wagon, making the emergency beef gather that his burnings had forced upon Cleve Anders. Maybe, he thought, that was where Anders was, too.

Well, he would watch here a while longer. The sun rose higher. He chewed a strip of jerky for breakfast and drank from his canteen.

The morning burned on. There was a contingent of guards still down there at the home ranch, three or four men with rifles; Anders was evidently taking no chances on Rae slipping in in broad daylight to start another fire. Or to hunt him down, Rae thought. But no. He became more and more convinced that Anders was not down there. By ten o'clock there had been no sign of him.

When the sun's position indicated an hour until noon, Rae finally stirred. He was sure now that Anders was not at the home ranch. Maybe he was out with the herd, maybe somewhere else. Rae thought for a moment; then, a decision made, he squirreled back up the slope to where the sorrel was tethered in the pines.

He had seen the wrangler take the horse herd out to grass just after breakfast, accompanied by an armed guard—Anders was taking no chances on *anything*. The *remuda* had crossed a ridge that would block it from sight of the home ranch and was fanned out in a swale, grazing. Now Rae rode a wide, cautious circle that would bring him up to it.

It took a half hour to get into position. When he was where he wanted to be, he tied the sorrel and went the rest of the way on foot, so that its presence would not attract attention from the herd and betray him. He moved like an Indian, taking advantage of every cover, and before long he was again at the edge of some timber, this time looking down into the swale where the *remuda* was a colorful scatter against the burnt brown of fall grass.

As he had hoped, both the wrangler and the guard had relaxed vigilance. They had dismounted and were sitting together with their backs against the same pine. Though the guard still had his rifle across his lap, he was more concerned with the two cans of tomatoes the wrangler was hacking open with a sheath knife.

It was a break; for once luck was on his side. Rae dropped into the tall grass and went as fast as he dared down the slope.

As he came up within earshot of guard and wrangler, he could hear their drowsy voices. The guard was saying, "I recollect one time in Cheyenne, this feller braced me in a bar—" His voice droned on, spinning a windy to pass the time, while he and the wrangler slurped the canned tomatoes.

Rae stepped out from behind his last cover and walked the final three paces upright, sixgun in hand. When he was behind them, his voice sounded loud, savage, in the noontime silence, even to him. "Freeze, both of you, or you're dead."

The wrangler jumped up, but the guard was an old hand. He did not move, did not even look around. He stayed exactly where he was, with the rifle across his lap.

The wrangler was only a boy, no older than Will; his eyes widened first in surprise, then in recognition. "It's Marsh."

The guard said dryly, "I figured. Don't ever jump like that when somebody's got the drop."

"You're a smart *hombre*," Rae said, stepping around in front of them, gun threatening both. "Now, real easy, throw that rifle away."

The guard grinned. "I never argue with a man with the hammer back and his finger on the trigger." He had the coolness of experience; he knew when he was beaten. He tossed the rifle away carefully.

"Now, your hoglegs. And knives. Both."

"Do what he says," the guard cautioned the wrangler.

"That's right," said Rae evenly. When both men were disarmed, he said coldly: "Now. You got jest one minute to tell me where Cleve Anders is."

For the first time, the guard batted his eyes. "Hell, I don't know," he said. "I jest work here. He don't tell me his plans."

"That's too bad," Rae said. The guard's face paled a little beneath a scraggly beard.

The wrangler stammered with fear. "Wait," he said. "W-wait. I—I heard Will say at chow this mornin' that Mr. Anders went up to Grand River City yesterday to see about hirin' more hands."

"When's he comin' back?"

"I—I don't rightly know. Sometime today, I guess. He was to meet Will out at the herd with the new hands . . ."

Rae smiled tightly. "Where's the herd?"

"They're gatherin' on the north range. On the flats up near Rock Creek."

"I see. All right." Rae's mind worked; he couldn't shoot these two in cold blood, but he couldn't turn them loose to give the alarm, either. He moved the gunbarrel in command. "You," he said to the guard. "Take your rope off the saddle and tie him up."

Slowly, cautiously, the guard got to his feet. He went to his groundhitched horse and unlatched the rope. Rae watched him keenly. But the man was in no mood to risk his life under a dead drop for a ranch that was just another way station in his hard-bitten career. Obediently enough, he went to the wrangler. "Hands behind his back?"

"That's right," Rae said.

The guard said, "Okay, Jake. Turn around."

Rae moved up close and watched as the guard bound the pale-faced boy. When the last knot had been tied, Rae said with grim humor, "Good job." Then, without warning, he swung the gun barrel, bringing it down hard on the guard's head.

The man crumpled and fell, out cold. Rae cut the leftover the rope that bound the wrangler and quickly hogtied the unconscious man. Then he tested the wrangler's ropes, tightened the knots.

"You'll be uncomfortable for a spell," he said to the frightened kid, "but you'll live through it. Long about nightfall, somebody'll wonder where the herd is and come lookin' for you." Then he tossed guns and knives far into the brush and hurried back up the slope to his own mount.

Though he'd had luck in getting information, there was no luck in the fact that Anders was gone and that when he came back he would not be alone, but surrounded by more guns. And that his destination was the herd, where there were even more men waiting to act as his protectors . . . even Will, Rae thought grimly.

But he was still possessed by that grim determination, and as quickly as he could, he worked his way around the rim of Circle M toward the north range.

Mid-afternoon found him in position above the flats, sheltered by a thick grove of pines. But he was nowhere near as secure here as he had been in his covert above the ranch house. Circle riders would be working the fire-scarred range, bringing in their gathers, and the area around the herd would be alive with men. He knew he must not relax his vigilance even for a moment.

Though he had not slept in nearly twenty-four hours now, the icy hatred that gripped him was a good enough substitute for sleep. He did not think he would ever sleep again until Cleve Anders was dead.

But, as the afternoon dragged on, Anders did not appear. The sun heeled down; some of the activity died, as more and more riders came in with the gather made on their second circle of the day. As they put their cattle into the herd, they rode up to the wagons where the cook was bent over his fire and dismounted. Generally, punchers on roundup took no food with them when they went out on circle; these men had not eaten since breakfast and they headed for the cold biscuits and hot coffee the cook always kept available.

Now the last riders were in with their cattle, and the shadows were lengthening. A skeleton guard held the herd, while the rest of the hands loped in to the wagon, where the cook was beginning to ladle out supper. Rae recognized one of the men around the fire, slender, gun-hung. Will. Young as he was, apparently he could pull his weight as range boss, and Rae could not help feeling a twinge of pride in him.

But damn it, would Anders never come?

He moved slightly, stiffly, in the hollow where he lay. And that was when he heard the sound in the pines behind him.

It was no more than a tick, a scrape, of the kind one limb might make against another. But there was no wind, and it triggered an instant reaction in Rae Marsh.

The short hair on the back of his neck rose, and he froze, head down.

He could not be sure, but he thought the sound came again.

Slowly, very slowly, and with infinite craft, he turned in his hollow, keeping his concealment, and peered up the slope. The pines were only a pool of shadow; now the wind had risen and they were soughing slightly, mournfully.

But his instinct warned Rae, there was somebody up there. Somebody who might already have discovered his sorrel. Somebody who would be looking for him.

He thought he saw one of the shadows in the pines move in a way an ordinary shadow had no business doing. He tensed and edged the gun barrel through the brush that concealed him. But the motion ended, and the woods were dark again, the fading light unable to penetrate the canopy of needled boughs.

Who was it up there—Anders? Had he spotted Rae? If so, why hadn't he attacked? Again Rae could feel the prickle at the back of his neck. He was in a deadly position—caught in a pincers, between whoever was above him and the roundup camp below him.

Then he sucked in his breath.

There was motion on the slope, an almost imperceptible movement of grass and brush. Someone was coming down the slope toward him, belly-crawling like a snake.

Rae eared back the hammer on the Colt.

The man passed by ten yards away, unaware of Rae's presence. When he had gained the shelter of a hump of ground, he opened a telescope and looked at the herd. Rae stared unbelievingly at the man's long form, sprawled flat against the earth. He was certain that this *hombre* was Tom Ford.

But there was no time to speculate. Ford scanned the herd briefly, snapped the telescope shut. Then he turned and began to crawl back up the slope. He was a shadow, soundless, and Rae marked his passage only by the faint movement of the grass until Ford regained the edge of the pines.

Then, in the gathering darkness, more shadows stirred.

And Rae knew now—Ford and his men were up

there in the pines. Apparently they had not spotted Rae; and somehow they must have missed his horse, hidden back there in a narrow gully. Their interest was in the herd below—the herd to which Anders had not yet come, the herd at which Will Marsh was gesturing even now, as he detailed men to relieve those holding the cattle.

Immediately, Rae realized what was happening.

Tom Ford had doublecrossed him. Either he had never meant to keep his promise about laying off of Circle M cattle, or he had been unable to resist the tempting prize down there on the flats—nearly five hundred head of prime beef. There could be no other answer—Ford was here to raid the herd, and Rae was caught between him and Circle M.

Rae bit his lip, filled with anger and bitterness. Evidently Ford had decided a herd of this size and quality was worth fighting for. Certainly there would be no other way he could get it. But he had planned cleverly to minimize the risk. Twilight was always the most relaxed, off-guard time at a round-up camp. Men were tired then, and hungry, thinking about food and rest, their reactions slowed, their senses dulled. Rae looked at the sinking sun. Even now, Ford and his men must be mounting up. Soon, he guessed, they would swarm down the slope, exercising the advantage of surprise for all it was worth.

And Will, Rae realized, would be caught right in the middle of all that. Will, with more guts than sense, proud of his gun-skill, would charge right into Ford's men and would be the first to go, with no more chance than a snowflake in hell.

Rae cursed bitterly, under his breath. Damn it, if

only Will were not with the herd . . .But Will was, and now a choice was being forced upon Rae.

Damn Ford—damn him for a promise-breaking, betraying, cold-blooded liar! He had sworn not to hit Circle M again!

Now shadows were definitely moving in the pines. There was no more time to think; Ford was gathering his men for the charge. It was either lie low and let them pass him by and hit the herd, killing right and left, killing Will, or else—

There was no other way to save Will. He had to give Circle M some warning, so they would not be hit off-guard. Rae was almost certain he could see the outline of mounted men at the edge of the pines.

Cursing softly to himself, he lined the Colt. Then he squeezed off three shots at that group of shadows, so quickly their reports strung together in a single, thunderous sound.

He had no chance to see what the reaction was down at the herd. The reaction on the slope was instantaneous.

But, knowing his gun flashes in the twilight would give him away, Rae had expected that. He was already rolling frantically across the ground as gunfire crackled from the edge of the pines and a hail of lead stormed across the place he'd occupied. If he had not been moving as soon as the last slug had cleared his gunbarrel, he'd have been cut in two.

As it was, the rip of bullets came hair-raisingly close. But it ended in an instant, and he was unhurt. A yell sounded from the edge of the pines: "Come on!" Then Ford's men were charging out, down the slope, two dozen of them, lashing their horses, holding their fire until they hit the herd.

Rae was directly in their path. A masked rider on a pounding mount loomed over him; it was move or be run down. Rae sprang to his feet, gun up. It went off seemingly of its own volition. He had an unforgettable glimpse of the surprise in the eyes above the mask as the man pitched backwards; then Rae was clawing for the horse's reins as it thundered past.

He barely snagged them; the charging animal dragged him ten feet before he pulled it around. Without touching foot to stirrup, he sprang into the saddle.

Most of Ford's men were by, then, pounding on down the slope, beginning to fire now as they went. Only one of them, who had seen his companion drop, wheeled his horse, swinging his gun towards Rae. With only two rounds left in the Colt, Rae fired blindly, instinctive snapshots, and the rustler was knocked from the saddle when both slugs caught him in the chest.

For the first time, Rae had a chance to see what was happening below.

The warning he had given Circle M, brief as it was, had made all the difference in the world. The blare of gunfire had brought them alert; as Ford's men came down in a firing wave, some of Circle M had already mounted. Others had sprung for shelter behind the wagon, with carbines ready for use. The dim light was shot with muzzle-flashes as gunfire crackled and spattered, Circle M meeting the attack with a fusillade of its own.

Rae could have turned his own horse, then, and

ridden clear. He never knew what it was that
dragged him into the battle. But later he thought it
must have been the sight of Will, disdaining cover,
out in plain sight, a perfect target, both guns blaz-
ing.

"You damned fool!" Rae roared. He dragged
shells from his belt, kicked the horse with spurs.
Even as it lunged down the slope, he was reloading.

The confusion below was total. The charge of
Ford's men, deprived of the advantage of surprise,
reached the foot of the slope in a ragged wave, then
broke against the wall of fire Circle M was throwing up. Horses reared and plunged, men yelled; in
the near-darkness, guns flashed brilliant orange.

Miraculously, Will was still on his feet. But he
fired his last round just as Rae's horse galloped
into the melee. Rae turned the mount towards
Will, who had begun to run for the shelter of the
wagon now, to reload.

But the kid's foolhardiness in staying exposed
was going to be the death of him. Rustler and cow-
hand alike swarmed in combat around the wagons
and the campfire now, and Rae saw a blackmasked
man lining a Colt down on Will, as the boy
plunged for shelter. The range was point blank and
there could be no missing.

Rae did not even try to hit the rustler with a
shot. The horse was a far bigger, surer target. His
slug punched into its flank, it squealed, reared, and
fell, and the masked man's gun fired straight up
before he vanished under the crushing weight of his
mount. Then Will had at least the shelter of the
wagon and was scrabbling cartridges into a Colt.

Rae was almost deafened by an explosion in his

ear. He turned to see another mounted rustler pumping slugs toward the wagon, and he dropped the man with a single shot. Then something slammed him with a mighty fist; the ground came up and hit him with terrible impact, and he was flat on his back in the scattered embers of the campfire, his whole left side numb from the slug he'd taken just below the collar bone.

He lay dazed for a second or two, as horses' hoofs, mostly bound in muffling bags, trampled across and around him. By some miracle, none landed on him. He realized he still had his Colt in his right hand, and he tried to pull himself up, but now everything was swimming.

Then, like something in delirium, a face showed above him in the fireshine, the face of a mounted man, mask pulled down now, teeth bared in a snarl. A lean, ferocious face, blade-thin and full of thwarted, killing fury. It was Tom Ford, and somehow Rae caught his shouted words in the screaming, thundering confusion that should have drowned them. "Marsh! You're the one was up there—" Ford's gun fell into line.

All time, all motion, seemed to be frozen then. What happened took place in the tick of a clock or less, but it seemed to Rae to take forever. He felt as if his Colt were coming up leisurely, as if he had all the time in the world. As if Tom Ford would wait upon his pleasure. There was no urgency in him and no doubt. He just pointed the gun and fired.

And Ford's face vanished in a wash of red and Ford's bullet plowed the earth beside Rae, and Ford's horse charged riderless across him, something bouncing, dragging, from one stirrup, and then a great weariness closed down on Rae Marsh. Whatever was happening, he could do no more. He lowered his gun, and then everything was very far away. Finally, there was only blackness in which he drifted.

XIII

"HE'S LOST A lot of blood," somebody protested, seemingly from the other end of the world.

"I don't give a hoot what he's lost," another voice snarled. "I want him awake."

Rae wanted to open his eyes, but the effort even of that seemed more than he could make. He realized vaguely that the voices were arguing over him, but he could attach no importance to their argument. His shoulder hurt, but not even the constant pain could penetrate the torpor that held him.

"I'm telling you again," the first voice said. "He wasn't one of *them*. Somebody fired warning shots before they hit us. If it hadn't been for those, we'd have been caught cold turkey. I think it was him. Because when he came in, he was the only one wasn't masked and he wasn't shooting at us. It was *them* he was fighting. I saw him knock one of 'em over just as he was about to burn me down."

The other voice grunted. "This was your first real fight. When you're older, you'll learn your imagination plays tricks on you. Hell, yes, he was one of 'em. He's always been one of 'em. And until we finally corpse him once and for all, we'll never have no more peace on this range."

Then somebody was shaking him, roughly, brutally. Pain from his shoulder lanced through him with fresh intensity; it brought him awake, yelling.

And it was daylight, gray dawn, and he was looking into the grinning, triumphant face of Cleve Anders.

"I thought that would bring you out of it," Anders chuckled. He was squatting beside Rae, his eyes glinting with pleasure and anticipation. "Well, buddy, you finally overreached yourself, didn't you? You've given us a right rough time of it; you've rustled and burned and murdered and every time we laid a hand on you, you've squirmed loose. But you're through squirmin' now, I'll guarantee you. You and your outfit didn't count on me showin' up with six new gunhands, did you?" He paused a minute, taking his makings from his shirt pocket. "Well, we got a right nice stack of dead rustlers here. And you'll jest fit on top of the pile."

He stood up and put his arm around Will's thin shoulders. "You bit off more'n you could handle when you tackled ole Will here and me. Together we make a real team, huh, Will?" He withdrew his arm and slapped Will on the back. "The boys tell me you handled them two guns like Billy Bonney hisself."

For a moment, Will's eyes glowed under this flattery, but then his face went serious again and he stepped a pace away from Anders. "It wasn't like I thought it was goin' to be," he said. "It was . . . it was a mess." His mouth twisted.

"Aw," Anders grunted, "you jest got buck fever now it's all over. This fight'll spread your name all over Colorado. And when they hear that you're the one finished off Rae Marsh, it'll spread a lot farther than that. You'll have that gunman's rep you've been hankerin' after so long. You'll be famous."

Will's eyes widened, his mouth dropped open. "Me?"

"Well," Anders said casually, "somebody's got to do it. And *I* ain't interested in buildin' up no rep." He shrugged. "Ever since you was so high, you've dreamed of nothin' but bein' known all over as a fast man with a Colt. This'll give you your chance."

Will just stood there.

"Listen," Anders snapped, "you ain't even thinkin' about that crazy claim of his that he's old John's son, too, are yuh? I tell, that's a bunko game, a cock-and-bull story. He ain't got no more of John Marsh's blood in him than I have!"

Will turned slowly and looked down at Rae.

"He's got my eyes," he said quietly. "And that letter—and it's Dad's handwritin'."

"That writin's so shaky nobody can tell whose it is," Anders scoffed. "And you're imaginin' that part about the eyes. He's a bunko artist that come in here and tried to run his game on us, and when that didn't work, he showed his true colors and went to rustlin'. Hell, if he was really John Marsh's son, why didn't John tell us about him? Why did he keep him a secret?"

"You know how Mom was," Will said. "So crazy jealous. She would have hit the ceilin' if she'd known he'd been married before." But he looked undecided, as if Anders' arguments were eroding his certainty. He was, after all, Rae thought sickly, only a kid, used to being under Anders' thumb, used to deferring to the older man, used to accepting his judgments.

"He's a rustlin', killin' wolf," Anders said harshly, "and he's gotta be wiped out like one, and his hide nailed to the barn door. Even if he was my kin, I wouldn't want to claim 'im. I wouldn't want the world even to think I had anything to do with a lobo like this 'un."

During all this argument, Rae's head had begun to clear; he could feel, with wakefulness, a measure of strength coming back to him. He wrestled himself to a sitting position, and as he did, Anders whipped out a gun and covered him.

"Even with one arm in a sling, he's dangerous as a snake," Anders rasped. "You can't take your eye off him fer a minute."

Rae looked around. He was next to the wagon in the Circle M camp. Out on the flat, he could see the herd. A few riders were still saddling up, and the cook was hunched over his fire a distance away; he and Anders and Will were out of earshot of all of them.

"Anyhow, if he can sit up, he can ride," Anders said. "A little piece. He won't have to ride but a little piece." He grinned at Will. "Come on. Let's git it over with, before this slippery bird thinks up some new trick."

"No," Will said. "No, we got to take him in. He's got to have a trial, and this matter of his third's got to be settled in court. Dammit, Cleve, we can't take this kind of thing on ourselves." He looked down at Rae. An edge of bitterness crept into his voice. "But you promised me the rustlin' would stop. We lost two good men last night."

"Ford doublecrossed me," Rae said shakily. "But I tried to give you warnin'. You look up there on the hill, you'll find another dead rustler. I plugged him as they were comin' down."

Will's face was still somber. "But what was you doin' up there in the first place? You give me another promise, remember? That you'd ride out of here, make no more trouble. How come you were up there watchin' the herd to begin with?"

Rae was silent for a moment. Then his eyes swiveled to Anders.

"I come to kill him," he said hoarsely.

He saw the shock that washed over Will's face. "After you made me that promise?"

Anders let out a roar. "You see? He's a lousy, bushwackin' skunk! And I'm through wastin' time. If you won't do it, I will." He reached down and grasped the slack of Rae's shirt. "On your damn' feet!" And he yanked Rae to his feet by main strength.

Rae gagged at the ferocious pain that swept through him, and the world seemed to go around and around. He leaned against the wagon for support, unable to speak.

"Bart!" Anders' voice boomed. "Catch up three horses an' bring 'em here."

Then he turned to Will. "I don't think we need any more palaver. You heard him say it with his own mouth."

Will rubbed his face, shielding his eyes with his hand for a moment. Then he let out a breath. "You're right," he said. "I've been a fool." He took his hand down, and now his face was fierce, merciless, as he looked at Rae. "I run up on him out in the back country yesterday. I could have burned him down then, and I was a sucker not to. But I thought ... I thought if he was my half brother, I ought to give him one last break. He promised me there'd be no more rustlin'. He promised me he'd clear out right away. And both promises broke. I'd have had a tighter guard out if it hadn't been for that promise."

Anders' voice was, for him, gentle, understanding, clinching Will tighter to his side. "Hell, you're still a young-un. Nobody blames you. The thing is, now we've got 'im and we got to handle him like he deserves and we ain't gonna waste no time about it. Here come th' horses."

He took the reins. "Bart, we're gonna escort this polecate on into town to th' law, where he'll git a nice, fair trial." He grinned. "But if you should hear a shot, don't let it spook yuh. After all, fix he's in, it's likely he'll try to escape."

The puncher, Bart, grinned back. "Sure," he said. "I know what you mean. After last night, one more shot ain't gonna spook nobody. And you shore don't want him gittin' away." He turned and strode toward the fire.

Anders jabbed Rae with the gun barrel. "All right. Climb aboard."

Rae just leaned against the wagon wheel, gasping with the pain of his wound.

"Hell, he's too weak to mount by himself," Anders said, swinging up. "Give him a hand, Will—but watch out he don't grab one of your irons." He kept the muzzle of his gun hard on Rae.

Will went to Rae and his hands were none too gentle. Rae dimly realized that Anders had planted a seed in Will that was building into bitter fury. Even if Will himself would not perform the execution, he would no longer object to it.

Rae shook his head. Damn it, if he could only think. If the pain would only stop, his brain only clear. But as Will tusseled him up into the saddle, the pain flared anew, making him gasp and cling to the horn, lacking any strength to resist.

Then the horse was moving, each step it took sending fresh agony through Rae. He could feel wet warmth in the bandage around his shoulder; his wound was seeping blood. It was all he could do to hang on.

"He's damned sick," Will said.

"That's all right," Anders said. "He ain't got far to go and he'll be outa his misery in a minute."

Then they were in a grove of pines. The horse stopped. Anders' voice said, from out of a blur, "This ought to be about right. I just wanted to git out of sight of the men. No use havin' any more waggin' tongues than anybody can help. Pull him down."

Rae felt Will's hands helping him. His feet touched ground, and he leaned against the bole of a big pine, gasping. A little of the pain went away now, or maybe he was getting used to it. He raised his head, focused his eyes with intense effort. Anders, gun out, was standing in front of him. Will a little to one side.

"Well," Anders rasped, "you wanta do it, or you want me to? Remember, this is your chance to git real famous."

Will's face was pale. He swallowed and licked his lips. "I—"

Rae summoned all his strength. "Wait," he croaked.

"Wait, hell," Anders said, thumbing back the hammer.

"No, wait," Will said. "He's tryin' to say somethin'."

"I don't want to hear anything he's got to say," Anders grated. But before he could pull the trigger, Will had stepped in front of the gun.

"Just hold your fire a minute," he said. "Let him say whatever it is—"

"Git outa th' way!" Anders roared in sudden fury.

"Cleve killed John Marsh," Rae husked.

"What?" Will turned, still shielding Rae. "What's that you said?"

"Ask Doc Miller. That's why I was comin' after him. He poisoned John Marsh with the dope John Marsh was takin'. Doc Miller knows. Crystal knows, too."

Will stared at Rae, then whirled. "What's all this?" he flared at Cleve.

Anders snorted. "Bellywash. That's what. John's heart failed."

"Lie," Rae snapped, his hatred for Anders greater than his pain or weakness. "John told Cleve . . . about me. Cleve killed him to keep him from seein' me, givin' me a third of Circle M. John was supposed to live sixty, ninety days longer. But Cleve was afraid I'd come before then."

"I've had enough of this," Anders roared. "Stand outa th' way, Will—for th' last time."

"No," said Will sharply. "No, there's not gonna be any execution. Not until I've talked to Doc Miller. Put your gun up, Cleve."

"The hell I will!" Anders shouted, and now his face was mottled with fury. Suddenly he thrust the gun forward. "Yes, dammit, I poured that stuff in John. Sure—but it was jest to put him outa his misery, the way you'd shoot a horse with a broken leg. He was bound t' die anyhow—why string it out?"

"Cleve." Will's voice was a shocked whisper.

But Anders' face was transformed now. It was a twisting, hating mask and his eyes were gleaming. "Well, dammit, you're not fool enough yourself to wanta give away half of what you own in Circle M to this joker—half of a fortune? Now stand aside or—or dammit, I'll blow a hole in you too and say he did it and then I'll own the whole spread, I won't hafta worry about either one of you! *Move!*"

But Will only stood frozen for a moment, staring incredulously at his step-brother. Then a cry came from deep within him, a cry of rage and grief, and suddenly he drew. His draw was miraculous; Rae had never seen its equal. The gun was in Will's hand as if by magic, and even as Anders pulled the trigger, Will's gun roared, too.

It was drawing and firing into a dead drop, and if Will had not been a miracle of gunswiftness, he would have been a dead man. But even though Anders' gun was out and cocked, Will's bullet ploughed home first by a fraction of a second, and though the two shots thundered almost simultaneously, the slug from Anders' gun whined off through the trees. Then Anders was clutching his belly, sinking to his knees, face contorted with agony.

He tried to raise the gun again, pointing it at

Will. "Damn you both," he choked. "Circle M shoulda been all mine."

Sobbing, Will watched Anders lift the Colt, slowly, weakly. Before it could come into line again, Will kicked out. The gun went flying, and Anders rolled onto his side, knees doubled up.

Then Will was on the ground beside him, tears streaming down his cheeks. "Cleve. You made me do it. Why . . .? Why . . .?"

Blood was coming from Anders' mouth; his voice was a fading, breathy croak. "Shoulda done for you th' same time I done for th' ole man. Mistake . . ."

But Will ignored that. "Cleve," he said again, and he cradled Anders' head in his lap. "Hell, Cleve . . ."

But Anders rolled away. He began to kick convulsively. It was a horrible thing to watch. At last his drumming feet slowed; then he sprawled motionless, eyes half-open, staring sightlessly. The gush of blood from his mouth slowed and died.

Will got to his feet, staring down in horror, his thin body trembling. In that moment, Rae wished he had strength enough to go to him. He knew what was happening inside Will. This was different, vastly different, from last night's battle.

Will turned slowly, his white face working. "He was all you said he was," he whispered. "But . . . I grew up with him. He was my brother, too." Suddenly, with a savage gesture, he hurled the pistol he held far into the pines. Then his left hand swooped down and drew the other gun and it went flying, too.

"Dammit!" he cried. "Dammit!"

Rae's eyes followed the flung guns; he could see

them gleaming in the underbrush. And along with the sympathy he felt for Will's anguish, a vast relief grew in him. This killing, Rae knew, would last Will all his life. There was no more gun-pride left in him and it would never come back. And that would be the kid's salvation.

The grim life and death of Cleve Anders had borne that much good fruit, anyhow.

XIV

THE SOUND that rang across the flats around the Circle M home ranch was as thunderous as gunfire.

But it was not gunfire; it was the banging of carpenters' hammers as a new house grew in a grove of cottonwoods away from the old one.

The old Circle M ranch house had been designed by a man for men; the new one, its fresh lumber gleaming in the morning sun, bore the more creative imprint of a woman's planning.

With his arm around Crystal, Rae Marsh stood there watching the builders. After so much bloodshed, so much destruction, he thought, it was good to see something being built.

Rae looked around the valley. Except for the noise of the hammers, it was quiet, sunlit, peaceful. And, he thought, half of it was his now. Legally. As one of John Marsh's two sons and heirs.

After the death of Cleve Anders, it had taken several weeks for Rae's wound to heal. He had spent those weeks in the Circle M ranch house, nursed unremittingly by Crystal. When he was up and about, there were court matters to tend to; he and Will told their stories in the court at Grand River City; Doc Miller sobered up long enough to testify; and the lawyers had their day. When it was over, everything Rae had fought for was his—a share of Circle M, Crystal, a chance to stop roving, stop fighting, put down roots and find some peace, some tranquility. He and Crystal had already set a date for their wedding, and a buyer had been found for her place in town.

And yet, except for Will, none of it would have come about. It had been Will who had insisted that Rae stay, instead of riding on after the healing of his wound, as Rae had been prepared to do. It had been Will who had seen to the court matters, and Will who had led Circle M men into Ford's place in the badlands and recovered most of the rustled cattle. Will was a man now, a man seemingly full-grown overnight. A man who accepted Rae Marsh wholly, unquestioningly as his blood brother.

And yet Will had not been quite old enough to absorb the shock of all that he had been through. No matter what Cleve Anders had been, he had been Will's brother, too, and though in those final minutes Cleve had cursed Will and been ready to kill him, Will could not forget that.

He had not emerged from that gunfight in the woods unscarred. He had withdrawn into himself, become grim-faced and moody. And there seemed nothing Rae could do to bring him out of it. Will's world had been blasted all to pieces, and though he was doing his best to put it back together again, he could not seem to make the pieces match.

Rae frowned now as he thought of that. It was the only fly in the ointment. Something had to be done to snap Will out of that depression before it turned him permanently sour, embittered him for life. Some way had to be found to heal the wound the killing of Cleve had ripped in his emotions without leaving a scar. But how? Rae had tried everything he knew, and it had all failed.

Crystal had not seemed as concerned about it as he, "Don't worry," she had said. "He'll come out of it. He's young. The young can take a lot."

But Rae had his doubts. The burden Will had to carry of grief, guilt and disillusionment would have been enough to destroy a man older and more mature than he. Now, as he scanned the valley, he expressed his concern.

"I hope this idea of yours works," he said. "He's been getting worse and worse."

"You worry too much," Crystal said. "Your shoulder healed, didn't it? That was because you had care and the right medicine. Well, Will's spirits will heal, too. All he needs is the right medicine."

"Maybe so," Rae grunted. Then he tensed. Hoofbeats drummed out on the flat; two riders appeared, pounding hard toward the home ranch. Rae squinted into the sun. "Here they come now."

Neither rider slowed; they galloped into the ranch yard neck and neck. Then Will drew his horse to a rearing halt. "It's a tie!" he yelled, and something leaped in Rae. Because, for the first time in weeks, there was mirth in Will Marsh's voice; for the first time in weeks, he was laughing, exultantly, happily.

Hallie, Crystal's young sister, was laughing, too. "I could have beat you if I hadn't been riding sidesaddle!"

"We'll try again tomorrow," Will grinned, and swung down. Then he reached up and took Hallie around the waist and helped her gently to the ground. For just an instant, their laughter died as they looked into each other's eyes; then it flared again. Completely oblivious to the presence of Rae and Crystal, they laughed as if they shared the finest joke in the world between themselves.

Crystal tugged at Rae's sleeve. "See?" she murmured. "Now, come on. Let's leave them to each other. I told you all it would take was the right medicine."

CHARTER BOOKS

SUSPENSE TO KEEP YOU ON THE EDGE OF YOUR SEAT

FROM THE NICK CARTER

KILLMASTER SERIES